D0480422

NOEL STREATFEILD'S Christmas Stories

Available in Virago Children's Classics

NOEL STREATFEILD'S

Christmas Stories

With illustrations by Peter Bailey

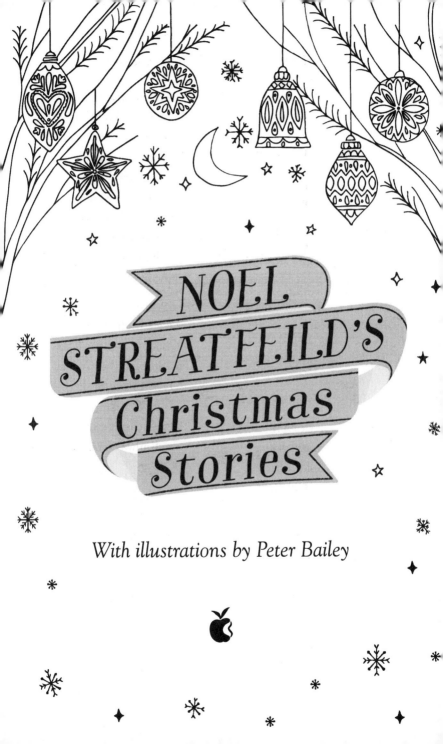

VIRAGO

This collection first published in Great Britain in 2018 by Virago Press

3 5 7 9 10 8 6 4 2

Typeset in Goudy by M Rules
Printed and bound in Great Britain by
Clays Ltd, Elcograf S.p.A.

Papers used by Virago are from well-managed forests
and other responsible sources.

MIX
Paper from
responsible sources
FSC® C104740
www.fsc.org

Virago Press
An imprint of
Little, Brown Book Group
Carmelite House
50 Victoria Embankment
London EC4Y 0DZ

An Hachette UK Company
www.hachette.co.uk

www.virago.co.uk

Contents

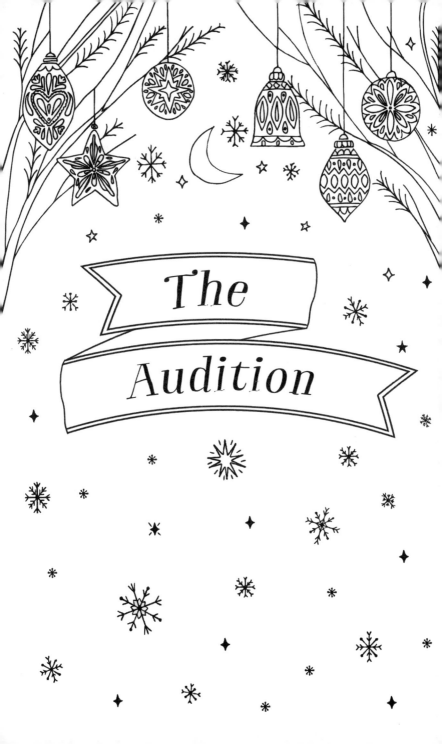

The
Audition

The twins were playing draughts: John in bed, propped up by pillows and Virginia curled up on the eiderdown. They were so engrossed they did not hear the door open and looked round surprised when the doctor spoke.

'Hullo, twins. Are you being nurse today, Virginia?'

Virginia gave the doctor the sort of smile which goes with liking somebody.

'Mummy's gone to fix some work being a guide to some visitors to London. The agency rang this morning.'

John knew the doctor was the sort of person to be pleased at other people's good luck. 'She might earn a lot of money.'

The doctor came round the bed. While he talked, he took John's pulse.

'What will she buy with it?'

The twins' father had been killed in a motor smash; he had left a little money, but there were such a lot of things that their income would not buy that when extra money came along it was a puzzle to decide what was needed most. Both twins took deep breaths so that they had plenty for the long string of things each thought the money should be used for, but John did not get a chance to speak, for the doctor put a thermometer in his mouth. Virginia walked round the room ticking off urgent needs on her fingers.

'There's a bill at the fishmonger's for special food while we both had measles; the fishmonger said he wasn't in a hurry but I know Mummy wants to pay. Then there's next term's fees at my dancing academy, but there's just a chance Madame might say we needn't pay because of me missing so much of this term with measles. Then John's got taller while in bed and good-ness knows if his clothes will fit, and truly I ought to have some new ballet shoes and . . . ' She broke off and looked at John who was making noises through his mouth shut round the thermometer. Nobody but a twin could possibly have understood what the noises meant. 'Oh yes, and John's just reminded me, Mummy said she simply must have some new saucepans and . . . '

The doctor took the thermometer out of John's mouth. He looked at it, his lips twisting in a half laughing, half miserable way,

'Seems there's a lot for that money to do.' He gave John's shoulder a pat. 'Taking your medicine?' John nodded. 'Good. Well, it's cold out, so stay in bed another day or two. Tell your mother I'll visit you again at the end of the week.' He put an arm round Virginia. 'Come and see me out, my little friend.'

In the hall the doctor put down his bag. He turned Virginia to face him. 'Can you tell me why you have quite got over your measles, but John, who had it no worse than you did, can't get strong again?'

'He hasn't the same things to get up for. I simply had to get well. Imagine getting measles the very day after you were twelve! Ever since I went to my dancing academy when I was nine I've been waiting and waiting to be twelve and have a licence, and it was more than flesh and blood could stand to be in bed missing auditions.' She lowered her voice. 'I've not told anybody, not even John, but I'm going to an audition this afternoon. It's for one of twelve in a ballet in *Puss in Boots*. That's why I'm not doing lessons this morning. Madame thought it might be too much after measles.'

'Quite right. I'll hold my thumbs for you. Hope you get it. I'll come and watch you if you do. But about John. Isn't there anything he likes, to pull him on to his feet again?'

Virginia sighed. 'Not really. You see he's what you'd call a one-dog boy, and since Frederick died, he hasn't liked anything much.'

'Wonder if I could get him a dog from the dogs' place at Battersea.'

'No, Mummy thought of that. They don't seem to have many stray dachshunds, and John only wants another dachshund. He says he doesn't, but he does. There's one called Charles in Mr Miggs's dog shop. He's not perfect because his eyes are the wrong colour, but he has the nicest little face. We first saw him the day before the measles started, and though we both felt peculiar, that dog nearly made us feel all right. He's still not sold. I see him often.'

'Expensive?'

'Terribly. Even with the wrong eyes ten guineas.'

The doctor picked up his bag. 'Wish I had ten guineas to spare. I'd give a lot to see John running about again.'

Virginia shut the door and went up to her bedroom thinking hard all the way. It had not until that moment struck her the doctor was worried about John. When she was thinking hard she practised dancing exercises. She held on to the end of the bed, turned out her toes and bent her knees. Suddenly she straightened up, her eyes shining. She rushed into John's room, pulling on her coat and beret.

'I'm going out for a little bit.'

Mr Miggs was a very old gentleman. He knew the twins well for they never passed his dog shop without looking in, and when Frederick was alive John had always lifted him up so that he could say how do you do to the other dogs. Mr Miggs was not a talking sort of man. He believed in gestures. He jerked a thumb at his window.

'Charles is still here.'

Virginia leant over the frame at the back of the

window. There was Charles, very young and gay and the colour of an autumn leaf.

'You lovely, gorgeous boy!' She came back to Mr Miggs. She lay half across his counter so as to get near to him. 'Today I'm going for an audition to dance in *Puss in Boots*. One of twelve in a ballet. Pantomimes run for weeks and weeks, and if I get chosen, even with Madame's percentage and what has to go in the Post Office for me, I'll earn much more than ten guineas. If I get the engagement, would you trust me and let me take Charles tonight? Dear, dear Mr Miggs, please say you will.'

Mr Miggs jerked his head towards Charles. 'Keep him for you.'

'That wouldn't be the same thing – you see . . . '

Out poured the story of John. Right from the beginning when their father had given Frederick to John as a sixth birthday present, through Frederick's illness and death – which Mr Miggs knew about already – up to the measles and what the doctor had said. Mr Miggs seemed stunned by hearing so many words, for it was a long time before he answered. Then he prodded Virginia's shoulder with a finger.

'Never trust anybody, but if you are engaged, trust you.'

Virginia slid off the counter. She was so pleased that her feet had to dance. She finished by throwing her arms round Mr Miggs and giving him a kiss. Mr Miggs was not a kissing sort of man. He rubbed his cheek where the kiss had been as if it had been a bite.

'Shut at five.'

'I know you do. I'll be here long before then.' Virginia leant over to Charles. 'Goodbye, loveliest Charles. You'll be walking home with me this very evening.'

The artists called to the audition were gathered round the empty stage. The dancing academy had sent fourteen girls. They all wore pink tunics, white socks and ballet shoes. They sat in a row trying not to look excited or nervous, but inside they all were, and nobody more so than Virginia. She must be engaged, she absolutely must. Imagine John's face when she walked in with Charles! The children had quite a while to wait. A lady sang 'We'll Gather Lilacs' and a man tried to show how funny he would be if he had on a cat's skin, and a fat girl recited Viola's willow cabin speech from *Twelfth Night* to show how splendidly she would say her lines if she might play the fairy queen. Then suddenly a voice from the stalls called, 'I'll see the children dancers now.'

The dancing academy had an audition ballet which they danced to the Sugar Plum Fairy's music. It had been designed by Madame to show a variety of steps and, as well, the ability of her pupils to keep in line and to keep time. Virginia, who was small for twelve, was in the centre. The ballet required all her concentration but at the back of her mind, beating like a tom-tom, was the word 'Charles! Charles! Charles! Charles!'

At the end of the ballet there was no sound for a minute. The girls stood about awkwardly waiting to be told what to do.

Then, after some whispering, a voice called, 'Will you each do a few steps separately.'

The school accompanist, who was at the piano, was expecting that order. Each girl had a short audition dance prepared. One by one they went through their steps. Virginia, watching them, clasped her hands and prayed, 'Oh God, don't let me slip. Do let me do my pirouettes perfectly.'

Virginia's turn came. She stepped forward. Suddenly alone in the centre of the stage she forgot Charles. She forgot everything except dancing. It was a divine feeling. When she finished, she had the lovely knowledge she had danced the very best that she could.

When all the girls had danced, there was a long, long silence. Then their own dancing mistress came to the orchestra rail. 'I want these twelve girls to stand forward.' She called out a list of names. Virginia felt her heart drop as if it was going down in a lift. Her name had not been called. She looked out of the corner of her eye at the other unlucky one. A red-haired girl called Elsa. They made faces at each other to show they knew their luck was out.

Then a voice called from the stalls: 'The twelve I have chosen can go. Now about that understudy . . . '

One last hope. Virginia gazed into the stalls. 'Oh, let it be me,' she prayed, 'Let it be me.'

'You with the red hair. I think you'll do nicely.'

Virginia was terrified she was going to cry. To cry at an audition! The shame of it! Madame would never forgive her. It would be no good telling Madame about

Charles. Madame would only see a child who had disgraced her school. She swallowed hard and blinked desperately. If only she could get her coat on and be alone somewhere. Oh, how a lump in the throat could hurt!

The accompanist got up from the piano and put an arm round her.

'Wake up, Virginia. They're speaking to you.'

Virginia blinked and came forward. She shaded her eyes from the lights and then saw a man leaning on the orchestra rail.

'You're quite a dancer, young lady. Could you recite something for me?'

All Madame's pupils had an audition recitation prepared. Virginia put her heels together, took a deep breath and began: 'You are old Father William . . . '

❄️

It was a miracle. It was something that had never happened to a girl from the academy before. To go to an audition to be one of a troupe of dancers, and be engaged to play the fairy queen! A fairy queen in a

white tu-tu who danced the Sugar Plum Fairy's dance!
The glory!

But Virginia's nicest moment was still to come. Mr
Miggs was waiting.

'Well?'

It was almost impossible to make Mr Miggs understand what had happened. He wasn't the sort of man

to know about fairy queens, and he had never seen the dance of the Sugar Plum Fairy, but he did understand the one thing that mattered, which was that the ten guineas was safer even than Virginia had hoped. Breathless with happiness, Virginia led Charles home.

John had spent a long, dull afternoon. He felt cross and tired. Suddenly the door opened. Something wriggling and red was in his arms and licking his face. He hugged Charles to him, feeling the hole left by Frederick filling right up. He was so happy he seemed swollen in front.

'Charles! It's Charles! Oh, Virginia, how did you get him? Oh, do you think you could telephone the doctor? Explain he's come. Explain I absolutely must take him for a walk tomorrow.'

The Bells Keep Twelfth Night

It rained and rained. It rained so much it was impossible to see the church from the Vicarage, which, seeing how close to each other they were, made Angus say, 'There's such monstrous rain coming down, there's absolutely no room between the bits.'

People coming in from the outside brought such a lot of water into the hall that Mrs Gage, who cleaned it, muttered, 'Ought to keep ducks, we ought. Reckon they'd do all right swimmin' round 'ere.'

The worst thing about the rain was that it came at the wrong moment. Before Christmas the children had been so busy with parcels, and decorating, and everything, they had no time to notice rain. Who would notice in the glory of Christmas what the weather was doing? On Boxing Day they had been to Uncle Alfred's pantomime party. On each day after that there was either a party or something going on in the parish, with which they had helped, and sometimes both. Then suddenly, all in a minute, Christmas stopped, and that was the moment when it had to be wetter than anyone could remember, and that was the moment when everybody began to notice that they had been eating more rich food than usual, and often staying up later than usual, and, as if a cork had popped out of a bottle, the accumulated results flew out, and all four Bells were black-doggish at the same moment.

On the second wet day, their mother, Cathy, who knew just how they felt, asked, 'Who can tell me what the date is?'

Ginnie stuck her chin in the air. 'Miss Virginia Bell can, it's January the sixth.'

'Twelfth Night,' said Paul.

Angus guessed what Cathy meant. 'Holly! We've got to take down the holly.'

'Not only the holly, but every decoration and every card.' Cathy saw nobody looked enthusiastic. 'And as a reward, after a picnic lunch of cheese and things, we'll go to a newsreel, and come home and roast chestnuts and play silly games and have high tea to make up for no lunch.'

The moment there was a plan, everybody stopped feeling black-doggish, and decided what they would do. Alex, the children's father, said he would see to the Christmas cards. 'I like to see there's no message on any of them that I missed in the rush of Christmas.'

Jane looked imploringly at Cathy. 'Could I help you undress the Christmas tree? Even though it means packing all the ornaments, I get a sort of Christmassy feeling just holding them before they go away.'

Paul knew his job. 'I'll get the ladder and take down the holly and stuff.'

Angus liked being on a ladder. 'And I'll help you and so'll Esau.'

Mrs Gage heard this. 'Esau's a good dog, no sayin' 'e isn't, but 'e's a bit off when there's a ladder about, upset it like as not. 'E'll sit in the kitchen along with me, won't you, duckie?'

Ginnie had listened to the family's plans in disgust. 'I suppose none of you remembered there was a Miss Virginia Bell and wondered what she'd like to do?'

Cathy laughed. 'Miss Virginia Bell can sort the paper, boxes and string the presents came in, and see what's worth keeping.'

Ginnie scowled. 'That's the beastliest job. Why should I do it?'

Alex did not like scowls. 'Why shouldn't you? Besides, it's a very important job. Do be careful there's no letter or message we've overlooked. It's so easy to miss something undoing a parcel.'

Ginnie, in a bad temper, sat on a stool surrounded by Christmas leavings. 'It's mean,' she muttered, 'A disgusting job! Folding bits of brown paper and winding up string. It's always me who has to do the worst things.'

Amongst the boxes Ginnie had to sort was a large square white one full of shavings. She recognised it. It had come from Miss Bloggs. Miss Bloggs was a wonderful parish worker, but not a favourite of the children's, in spite of the fact that she was a good and imaginative present-giver. This Christmas was the only present-giving time when she had failed. She had sent eggs. Eggs were scarce, and Cathy said, 'a gorgeous present'. But even though it's gorgeous to have a boiled egg for breakfast, it's not the sort of present you expect from someone who in the past, besides sending a grown-up present, has given a box full of indoor fireworks, a toy theatre and a ping-pong set.

Ginnie made a face at the box. 'It may think it's a good box,' she thought, 'but I'll show it what I think.' She got up and jumped. Squish, squash went the cardboard. She picked up the paper shavings and tore and tore until they were like bits of confetti. Smashing and tearing made Ginnie feel better. She skipped off the scattered remains and settled down to her sorting in a much better mood.

By twelve o'clock, the Twelfth-Night clearing-up was finished. The tree was as bare as when it lived in

a forest. The hall, without its holly and paper rings, had the shorn look of a boy when the barber has cut his hair too short. The mantelpiece and bookshelves looked like a garden when plants have been cut back – much tidier, but far less gay. As a result of Ginnie's work, the cupboard into which the Christmas mess had been pushed was empty, the chest in the hall where paper, string and boxes lived was full, and the wastepaper sack was bulging.

The picnic lunch was fun. It was eaten like a real picnic, sitting on the ground, and that made the bread, cheese and remains of Christmas taste special. Esau liked the picnic idea. He was not supposed to have snacks at meals, but when people sit on the floor to eat, bits come naturally to a dog, without grown-ups noticing. They had just finished eating when the telephone rang. Alex got up.

'Sure to be for me, so I may as well answer it.'

The children always listened to the beginning of telephone conversations in case it concerned them. This obviously did not, for they heard Alex say, 'Hello Miss Bloggs. When did you get back? Have a good Christmas?'

'I wouldn't think she did,' said Angus. 'I would think she felt mean inside only sending us eggs.'

Cathy hated the children to be grasping. 'What a horrid thing to say. Eggs are a lovely present, and it was terribly kind of her to give them to us.'

Jane patted Cathy's knee. 'You have to say that, but if you weren't speaking as a mother, you'd admit you were surprised there wasn't something for us four. There always has been.'

Alex came back. He looked at Cathy. 'What did Miss Bloggs send the children for Christmas?'

The children answered. 'Eggs.'

'Eggs.' Alex sounded puzzled. 'Eggs?'

'It was eggs,' said Cathy. 'Why?'

'She said she hoped the children would enjoy their present this afternoon.'

There was a puzzled silence.

'I suppose she thinks we eat eggs on Twelfth Night,' Angus suggested.

Jane jumped up. 'She never would. She must have sent something else.'

Cathy turned to Ginnie. 'There was nothing extra in the box the eggs came in, was there?'

Ginnie felt her face turning red. She looked at the carpet. 'No.'

Paul got up. 'We can easily see. The box wasn't broken, so it'll be in the chest.'

Ginnie saw she had to confess. 'It isn't in the chest. I threw it away.'

'Why?' Jane asked. 'It was quite good. It only wanted the shavings turned out.'

Ginnie was bored with the box. 'If you want to know, Miss Virginia Bell stamped on it and tore the shavings to pieces. It's all in little bits in the wastepaper sack. I did it because I was angry with Miss Bloggs because of the eggs.'

Cathy took command. 'Jane, get the dust-sheet. Paul, fetch the wastepaper sack. You might ask Mrs Gage to come and help. If it's something for the afternoon, we've got to hurry!'

There is nothing more difficult to search than a wastepaper sack. This was a particularly bulgy one, and it seemed full of everything except something from Miss Bloggs.

'If only we knew what we was lookin' for,' said Mrs Gage. 'But it might be anythin'.'

'I imagine it's a note,' said Alex. 'An invitation card or something of the sort.'

Cathy rummaged amongst the scraps of paper. 'It must be in those shavings, if only we could find them in all this mess.'

Angus made the first discovery. He held out a small piece of paper to his father. 'Could this be a bit of it? "ow K".'

The family gathered round. Mrs Gage was the first to guess what 'ow K' meant. 'It's theatre seats. Reckon she give seats for a theatre.'

With a howl, Jane flung herself amongst the paper shavings. 'Theatre seats! Oh Ginnie! Probably the most gorgeous matinee and we're missing it.'

Cathy looked pleadingly at Alex. 'Couldn't you ring up Miss Bloggs and say we missed the tickets? I expect the theatre would let the children use duplicates.'

Alex shook his head. 'She's not at home. She rang up from a friend's.'

Jane made the next find. Number 16. Then Mrs Gage had a triumph. She got the name of the theatre.

'We aren't 'alf gettin' on. Go and get the paper, young Angus, and see what's on. May as well know what you're missin'.'

The play was *Treasure Island*. Angus stamped with impatience when he knew. 'We must find the bits. If we aren't there early we'll miss Pew.'

Mrs Gage got up. 'I'll get a sheet of paper and make some paste. As you find the bits I'll stick 'em together.'

Little by little, the scraps of paper turned up. Bits of numbers. Bits of the figure 'K'. Bits of the word 'matinee'. Bits of the name of the theatre. When parts of all four tickets were assembled, Cathy sent the children up to get ready.

'We'll find the rest. If you hurry, you'll just make it. Such luck we ate at twelve.'

In spite of Mrs Gage's work with the paste, they were odd-looking theatre tickets.

'I'm not sure they'll let you in on these,' Alex said. 'You'll have to go to the box office manager and explain.'

Ginnie took the tickets. 'If you don't mind me saying so, nobody is going to explain except me. I tore them up and it's my right to say so.'

❄

They reached the theatre with five minutes to spare. Paul asked an attendant where the box office manager lived. The attendant pointed to a door next to the box office. Pityingly, the other three looked at Ginnie.

'If you like . . . ' Paul started to say.

Ginnie was not going to show she was afraid. 'I wouldn't like, thank you. Miss Virginia Bell will do her own dirty work.'

In an incredibly short time Ginnie was back, and with her was a tall, grey-haired man. He smiled at the family. 'Come on, I'll show you the way.'

The manager not only showed them the way, but gave each of them a free programme, and when after a gloriously exciting first act they came back to the everyday world, a waitress brought four ices with the compliments of the management.

Paul, Jane and Angus looked in an unusually polite way at Ginnie.

Paul whispered, so that nobody round him could hear, 'What on earth did you tell him?'

Ginnie slowly and luxuriously swallowed a large spoonful of ice-cream. 'I just explained.'

'But wasn't he cross?' Jane said.

Ginnie looked proud. 'Not a bit. If you want to know, we didn't discuss tickets. We discussed me being given mean jobs to do. He said he'd suffered that way himself, and this afternoon he'd see I was treated like a queen.'

The others eyed each other. It was a bit much, Ginnie getting away with it like that, after tearing up the tickets.

Paul whispered, 'Very decent of him, after you doing an idiotic thing like that.'

Ginnie finished her ice. She lay back in her seat in a grand way. 'If anybody's rude, I won't tell them the best thing.'

Jane nudged Paul. 'She did get us free programmes and ices.'

Paul grinned. 'I didn't mean anything.'

Ginnie took a deep breath. 'The seats weren't for this afternoon. Miss Bloggs made a mistake. We're all coming again tomorrow.'

The family gasped. Ginnie held up a hand. 'Now, stop talking. Miss Virginia Bell is going to read her programme.'

The
Moss Rose

Lavinia was wedged so tightly between the passengers on the Underground train that however much the coaches swayed, it made no difference, she just could not fall over. Not only was she squashed by passengers, but by parcels and suitcases. The parcels, even though they were wrapped in paper, trumpeted news of what was in them, and what day it was. The foot of a turkey brushed Lavinia's cheek. A large square box marked 'fragile' did not need to be opened to see the glittering Christmas tree ornaments inside it. What else could be travelling in a basin-shaped package on Christmas Eve but a plum pudding? Christmas Eve has a special feeling all its own, a mixture of excitement hustle and bustle. 'Even the suitcases look Christmas Eve-ish,' thought Lavinia. 'You can see they're lumpy because there are presents inside them, as well as clothes, but I bet nobody's got a more exciting suitcase than me.'

The thought of her suitcase made Lavinia forget the train and even Christmas Eve, for in her suitcase were her skates and boots. There was not a great deal of money in Lavinia's family, and there were two brothers to keep as well as herself; it had been the proudest moment of her life when she had come strutting home from the rink five weeks ago, able to tell her family that she was engaged as one of the skating girls in *Beauty and the Beast* on ice. It had been a special honour because the other girls were grown-up and she was only fourteen. The management had not wanted to use anybody not grown-up, but when they had seen her skate they had decided they must have her, because she would make such a perfect understudy for the Moss Rose. Of course, in the story of *Beauty and the Beast*, there had to be a Moss Rose, and because of the Moss Rose, a Rose ballet, and amongst the other Roses, the Moss Rose had to be noticeably the smallest.

A little Swedish star was the Moss Rose and, although she was grown-up, she was no taller than Lavinia. Today there had been the final dress rehearsal before the show opened on Boxing Day, and it was then the exciting thing happened. The little Swedish star had received a telegram calling her back to Sweden, so she, Lavinia, had skated in her place. In her mind, Lavinia tried to recall anything that anybody had said, how the dress had felt, how the steps had gone, so that she might repeat every single thing to the family as soon as she got home.

The Underground gave a sudden extra lurch and people started to surge out. 'Must be Earl's Court,' thought Lavinia, coming back to the Underground with a start, 'I must pay more attention or I'll get taken past my station.' The crowds jostled out and as they went they left more space. Lavinia thankfully gave herself a little stretch. She uncramped her fingers and put her case on the floor. She leant against the partition. It was all very well to tell yourself not to dream, but when you had been allowed to be the Moss Rose and just might be going to skate the role on Boxing Day, it was almost impossible not to dream. She could see the family's excited faces. She could hear the pride in her father's voice and the pleasure in her mother's. It was lucky the family had seats for Boxing Night as it would have been too awful if she was the Moss Rose and they never saw her.

She smiled down at her little case. All the cases of all the people would be full of exciting things on Christmas Eve, but what could be more exciting than the white boots and skates of somebody who might be going to skate as the Moss Rose in the Rose ballet? Carried away with a vision of herself in the role, Lavinia nearly forgot to get out at South Kensington. Luckily, several other people had to get out, and as they pushed by her one of them said 'South Kensington'. She came back to the Underground with a start, snatched up her case, and hurried up the platform.

Lavinia's father, Mr Ward, had managed to get hold of three rooms in a converted house. This meant there was a room to live and cook in, a room for the two boys, and a room for Mr and Mrs Ward. Lavinia slept in the living room. Often Mr and Mrs Ward thought rather miserably about their three rooms, and talked of the days when Mr Ward's ship would come in and they would have a little house with a garden, outside London. Sometimes even Lavinia and her elder brother Jock and her younger brother Jim thought the three rooms rather miserable, for they could not feel hopeful about their father's ship coming in because Mr Ward was a salesman in a hardware store, and it takes a long time for salesmen's ships to come in. But nobody, not the most cantankerous person in the world, could have thought the three rooms miserable that night when Lavinia came home. Paper rings hung everywhere, there were clusters of balloons, every single picture and ornament that would take it was supporting holly, and in the passage there was a great big bunch of mistletoe. At the far end of the living room there was a screen. Jock, Lavinia and Jim were on their honour not to look behind the screen, but even without looking behind you could not help seeing a tiny point of tree sticking over the top, and on the floor around the screen there were pine needles. As well, though of course this could be only guessed at, there would be the presents piled up around the little tub that held the tree, each in different coloured paper, and each with somebody's name written on it.

When Lavinia came rushing up the stairs and into the living room, she was greeted by a roar of singing. She was the last to come home, and Jock had planned that she should have a big welcome because once she was inside and the door shut, Christmas had really begun. He stood on a chair and conducted the family.

Christmas is coming,
The geese are getting fat,
Please to put a penny
In Lavinia's hat.

Lavinia pulled off her beret, threw it on a chair, put her suitcase on the ground and dramatically threw out her arms. 'I suppose you all think you're looking at just one of the skaters in *Beauty and the Beast*, but you aren't. You're looking at somebody who's most likely going to dance as the Moss Rose on Boxing Day!'

Everybody asked questions at once so that Lavinia had quite a job making herself heard, but at last she managed to get silence. She explained about the Swedish skating star, who had in some way broken a film contract by coming to skate in *Beauty and the Beast* and had to fly back to Sweden to get things settled. She might be back on Boxing Day, but it was thought more likely that she might not. Lavinia described the morning rehearsal, how she and the other girls had just started their first routine when the music had stopped and a voice had called through

36

the microphone, 'Is Lavinia Ward there?' She gave a description of herself hurrying to the manager's office, tripping over her skates because she was so excited, of how nice he had been, and of how she had then gone to the Wardrobe to try on the Moss Rose dress, which was the most gorgeous dress anybody had ever seen – a ballet dress of rose petals, but all shut in by green net like a proper moss rose. How the dress had

fitted perfectly, only needing a little bit of alteration to the bodice because she did not stick out as much as the Swedish film star.

Then she turned, beaming, to her mother. 'Imagine, Mum, I've always thought the wardrobe mistress very cross, but today she was so nice nobody could have been nicer. She said "Won't your Mum be excited when she hears you may be going to star on the first night?" And then she opened a drawer and she took out a moss rose petal, and she said "You take it home and give it to your mother so she can see what you're going to wear."' Lavinia knelt down by her case. 'I've put it away carefully in a piece of paper.' She unclipped her case, 'It's in the corner . . . '

Lavinia's voice had tailed away in so odd a fashion that it drew all the family round the suitcase to see what was the matter. What they saw was enough to make anybody's voice tail away for ever and ever. Instead of the white boots and skates that should have been there, there was the week's rations for one, a piece of cold chicken in greaseproof paper, a man's brush and comb, and a little parcel done up in coloured paper and ribbons.

It took some moments before the full horror of what had happened began to dawn on the family.

Jim was only ten and he liked his facts straight. 'How could you have taken somebody else's case? Weren't you holding yours?'

Mrs Ward shut the case and looked at the outside. 'Same brown exactly. No name on it, of course.'

Mr Ward was methodically going through the things in the case. 'And no name anywhere, nor likely to be I suppose. After all, who puts his name on his brush and comb.'

Jock was looking at Lavinia. 'They're your only skates and boots, aren't they?'

Lavinia nodded, tears dripping down her nose. Jock turned to his family, his voice was ferocious. 'We've got to find the beastly man, and make him hand back Lavinia's case. Even if we had the money we couldn't buy her any skates and boots because everything will be closed till after Boxing Day.'

Lavinia choked. 'And if I don't have my skates and boots I can't skate even as one of the girls in *Beauty and the Beast*. It's too awful. It would happen on the only day of my life when I had a chance to be the Moss Rose.'

Mr and Mrs Ward thought everybody would be able to discuss the frightful thing that had happened better if they had some food inside them. Lavinia knew she would never be able to eat any food again, and Jock was inclined to agree with her, but Mr and Mrs Ward were right. It was a specially nice meal, with real farm eggs sent as a Christmas present to Mr Ward from someone who worked in his hardware store, and it was extraordinary how easily a farmhouse egg, followed by a mince pie, went down, even at a time of unutterable grief. It was not until the meal was nearly over that Mr Ward began seriously to discuss the suitcase problem.

'Would you say, Lavinia, that whoever had your suitcase would have got out at South Kensington, the same as you?'

'Think, dear,' said Mrs Ward, 'when did you last see your own?

Lavinia shut her eyes and tried to remember. 'It was after Earl's Court . . . I didn't put it down till then . . . I saw it after that because my foot was against it . . . '

Jock leant across the table. 'Can't you remember somebody else having a case like yours?'

Lavinia screwed up her eyes tighter than ever. 'Left, standing near me after Earl's Court, there was a fat lady in a tweed coat, but it couldn't have been her because she had a string bag with a plum pudding in it in one hand, and parcels and parcels in the other hand, and her handbag. She never could have carried a suitcase too. There was a father with two little boys, but they'd been to one of those shops where you get a present from Father Christmas for a shilling. The little boys had enormous parcels, and the father was taking home the Christmas tree ornaments in one hand and in the other he was carrying the Christmas tree, so he couldn't have carried the case. Then there was . . . ' she broke off. 'The old gentleman with the turkey! It was in a parcel and its foot scratched my cheek. But in his other hand he did have a case, I'm almost sure he had a case, and that it was like mine.'

Mr Ward rapped the table for silence, for all the family were speaking at once. 'Could you describe what he looked like, and whether he got out at South Kensington?'

Lavinia frowned, trying to remember, then her face lit up. 'I know. He looked just like Father Christmas, only of course he wasn't wearing the right clothes, and he did get out at South Kensington, because he said Merry Christmas to the ticket collector, I know I heard him.'

Mr Ward got up from the table. He looked solemnly at the old gentleman's suitcase. 'I never touched anything that didn't belong to me in all my days, but this time it looks as though I'll have to. I'll have to open that little parcel, for all it's done up so nicely, for it may be a clue.'

'It's for his sake as much as for Lavinia's,' said Mrs Ward. 'Imagine the poor old gentleman with no rations, nothing but boots and skates.'

There is something shocking about opening somebody else's Christmas parcel, even when the opening is done from the highest motives. Mr Ward untied the ribbon and took the paper off the parcel as if he were expecting a wasp to fly out. Inside the paper there was a little box. Inside the box there was first of all a card with 'To dear little Emily with love' written on it, and underneath, a small tie-pin with a turquoise set in it. The pin was fastened to a piece of card, on which was written that turquoises were the lucky stone for people to wear who were born in December.

Jock looked at the clock. 'That settles it, Dad. We ought to he able to find those boots. It isn't eight yet – hours and hours to Boxing Day afternoon. There can't be so many little Emilys born in December. Most likely the old gentleman's her grandfather staying for Christmas. I'll go round and tell the scoutmaster. There's scouts all over South Kensington. We ought to have the case back in half an hour, shouldn't wonder.'

'That's the ticket, son,' said Mr Ward, 'and I'll go to the police station.'

But the case was not back in half an hour, nor was it back by dinner time on Christmas day, though it was not for want of trying. The police promised to let the Wards know the moment there was news. Jock's scoutmaster rang other scoutmasters, and they rang the guides, and the guides rang Brown Owls, until finally there did not seem to be a street within miles of South Kensington where somebody was not asking, 'Do you know a little girl called Emily whose grandfather is staying with her for Christmas, whose birthday is in December?'

It was, of course, a miserable Christmas for the

Wards, Lavinia tried hard, but it was no good pretending she was not getting more miserable as every second passed. She only picked at her piece of roast goose, and never bothered to look whether she had a threepenny bit in her slice of plum pudding. It was seeing this that made Jock decide that a final effort must be made. Soon it would be dark, time to light the Christmas tree. For weeks they had been working and planning for the Christmas tree; it must not all be spoilt when somewhere there was an old gentleman just as keen to get rid of a pair of white boots and skates as Lavinia was to have them back.

'Dad,' he said, 'do you know anybody who would lend a car?'

'What for?' asked Mr Ward.

'I'm going to make a megaphone. We'll broadcast for the old gentleman.'

The car went slowly up one street and down the other. Mr Ward, very red in the face because he did not like making himself conspicuous, sat in front by the driver, shouting through a megaphone. In the back were Jock, Lavinia, and Jim. Mrs Ward had refused to come with them.

'I'll get the tea, dears. You'll need something hot when you get in.'

'Lost, a suitcase containing white boots and skates. Found, a suitcase containing rations and small parcel with turquoise pin for little Emily.'

Heads popped out of windows; people ran to the front doors. Some laughed and said it was for all the world like an election campaign. Others got cross and told Mr Ward that was no way to behave on a Christmas Day, frightening people out of their lives, making then think that the water had been cut off or something. Mr Ward grew more and more ashamed and would have liked to give up, but the children prodded him in the back every time he stopped broadcasting and the owner of the car, Mr Smith, nudged him with his elbow.

'I've given up my Christmas afternoon for this jaunt. You keep at it, old man.'

It was four, it was half past four, it was five o'clock and quite dark. It was past tea-time. It was nearly Christmas tree time.

Mr Smith spoke apologetically. 'Sorry, old man, but I'll never hear the last of this from my missus if I don't get home soon. The kids have their tree at five and we've all the relatives coming this evening.'

Lavinia was past speech. Everything had been tried, it was no good going on, there was nothing left for it but to face the dreadful tomorrow when she had to go to the management and explain she could not skate because she had neither boots nor skates. Jim, though he was very sorry for Lavinia, had a big appetite and he knew there was a Christmas cake for tea. He thought there was very little more anyone could do, and he could not help thinking Christmas cake would comfort anyone, even Lavinia. Jock did not give in so easily. He was miserable for Lavinia and miserable for them all. Christmas only came once a year and took a lot of looking forward to. It seemed dreadful that it should be a spoilt day when it came, but even he had to give in. Everything that could be done had been done. He saw Lavinia could not speak, so he spoke for her.

'That's all right, Mr Smith. Lavinia says it was grand of you to help. She agrees it's no good trying anything else. We're going home.'

Mr Smith drove the Wards to their door. He had tried to think of something cheerful to say as he left them, but he failed. Driving them round, he had come to appreciate the full tragedy for Lavinia, and he knew anything he said would sound out of place. Instead, he patted her on the back and drove away in grieved silence.

Mr Ward put an arm around Lavinia. 'Look dear, we've done all we can, and I'm afraid it's all been to no purpose. Now I want you to make an effort. You know the trouble your mother's been to for Christmas, do you think you could try and pretend, just for the Christmas tree?'

Lavinia swallowed. With her fingers, she pushed up the corners of her mouth into something almost like a smile. Making a smile, even an artificial one, helps. After a moment her voice came back. She whispered, 'I'll try. Let's go in.'

The table was laid for Christmas tea. There were crackers and the Christmas cake and sandwiches. There was a big fire blazing, and the kettle was boiling. But there was no Mrs Ward. The smile Lavinia had fixed on her face for her entrance began to slip. Mr Ward seeing this shouted as cheerfully as he could, 'Mother! Mother! We're home.'

Nothing happened for a moment. Then, slowly, the far door that led to Mr and Mrs Ward's bedroom creaked open. Steps shuffled forward, then, weighed down by a sack, into the room came Father Christmas. After all the anxiety of the day, and the cold, fruitless drive round the streets, Father Christmas was the last person Mr Ward wanted to meet.

'What's this, Mother?' he called crossly. 'We've had no luck, and we want our tea.'

Jock too thought this was no minute for Father Christmas to arrive. 'Where are you, Mum? Lavinia's cold.'

Jim was delighted to see Father Christmas, but not before he had eaten. He sat down firmly at the table. 'We're awfully glad to see you, but we're hungry. Do you mind if we have our presents after tea?'

Lavinia had been staring at Father Christmas as if she were seeing a ghost.

Suddenly she gave a cry and flung herself at him. 'It's him! It's him! It's my old man.'

What a Christmas evening it was. The more glorious because the day had been so unhappy. The Christmas tree, from being a small tree in a tub seemed to grow until it reached the sky. Every ornament and candle glittered like the stars of the Milky Way. The presents, which had been simple, became the richest and grandest in the world, The centre of all the fun and laughter was the old gentleman. Over and over again he was made to repeat his story. How shocked he had been to find he had only boots and skates to eat for Christmas. How he had not been able to get out in the morning because he lived alone and had his housework to do, and a bit of yesterday's leftovers to cook for his dinner. But as soon after dinner as he could, he had gone to the police station. He did not get further than that before the family chimed in, Mrs Ward describing how he had arrived with the case soon after they had gone out, and how in her old dressing gown she had rigged him out as Father Christmas.

Jim had to break in there.

'Which he really is.'

The old gentleman nodded in a pleased way. 'Every Christmas regular at Parkinson's Stores. "Christmas has come," the staff say. "Here's little Emily." That's their joke on account of my name being Emile.'

Jock laughed at that point. 'Imagine us all asking

about a little girl called Emily, and it was you all the time.'

The old gentleman looked proudly at his pin. 'They only see me in December as Father Christmas. That's why they've given me a turquoise. Nice of them to think of me.'

That made Lavinia miserable. 'Your only present, and you nearly never had it, and it's all my mistake for picking up your case instead of mine.'

The old gentleman chuckled. 'But look what it's brought me. For years I've spent Christmas on my own.'

Mrs Ward did not like that. 'But you never will again. You've us now.'

After all the presents had been opened they sat round the fire eating nuts and drinking ginger wine. Mr Ward lifted his glass to Lavinia's skates and boots which were in a place of honour on the mantelpiece.

'Here's to them, and to their success tomorrow.'

Mrs Ward turned to the old gentleman.

'And to the friend they've brought us.'

'Next Christmas,' said Lavinia, 'we'll know you're coming and we'll have a present for you.'

The old man felt in his pocket. He took something

out and held it up for them all to see. 'I had my present this morning. Done up in a bit of paper, and the moment I opened it I could feel luck come into my room.'

He held out a scrap of crimson satin.

Lavinia jumped to her feet. 'How gorgeous. I'd forgotten all about it. It's a petal of the Moss Rose.'

Thimble

John, Judy and Jennifer had their clothes made by Mrs Widgery. Snip, snap would go Mrs Widgery's scissors, and under the table would fall bright little bits of silk, fragments of muslin and pieces of striped cotton. Mrs Widgery would say, 'Let them lie. Royal robes for a royal cat.'

Mrs Widgery's cat was royal because his great-grandparents had come from the Royal Palace in Siam. The cat's name was Thimble. Not a very suitable name for a royal cat, but for Mrs Widgery, being a dressmaker, things in a work-basket came first to her.

Thimble was a lovely little cat, with markings the colour of winter trees and dead leaves, and eyes as blue as morning glory flowers. It must be confessed, though, that when he spoke, he had rather a loud harsh voice, but that only showed his royal blood. Loud, harsh voices were hereditary in his family.

John, Judy and Jennifer, when they went to fittings for their frocks or for John's shirts, would peep under the table at Thimble. They never actually saw him dressing up in Mrs Widgery's snippets, but they often saw him gaily tossing little pieces of material into the air. Once, Jennifer caught him with a fragment of yellow muslin in his mouth and she knew, if only she had been able to look one second longer, she would have seen him twist it into something gorgeous and very, very royal, but at that moment Mrs Widgery, her mouth full of pins, said, 'Stand up, Jennifer, or this dress will never hang right.'

It was in the autumn that Mrs Widgery became ill. She would not at first admit how ill she was. She tried to sound her usual self and, between coughs, snip, snap went her scissors and she wheezed, 'Let the pieces lie. Royal robes for a royal cat.'

But it was no good pretending. The cough got worse and worse until one day an ambulance drove up to Mrs Widgery's door, and into it she was carried, and away she went to the hospital.

The next day something else drove up to Mrs Widgery's door. It was a taxi. Out of the taxi got a severely dressed, scraggy woman, whose eyes darted about as if looking for specks of dust. It was Mrs Pim, Mrs Widgery's sister-in-law, who had come to look after the house and Thimble while Mrs Widgery was in hospital. From behind the curtains in Mrs Widgery's street, the neighbours peered at Mrs Pim and at once they all said the same thing: 'Poor Thimble! She's not the type to understand a royal cat.'

John, Judy and Jennifer heard about Mrs Pim. They called at the house the very next day, partly to ask if Mrs Widgery was better, but mostly to see how Mrs Pim and Thimble were getting on together. Mrs Pim did not like children; she had a face that said so. It was the sort of face that made John, Judy and Jennifer forget what they wanted to say. In the pause, while they tried to remember, Mrs Pim asked in a voice which sounded like the click of Mrs Widgery's scissors, 'Well?' John said: 'How is Mrs Widgery today and ...' but before he could enquire how Thimble was getting on Mrs Pim snapped, 'As well as can be expected,' and she shut the door.

Although they tried very hard, it was a week before the children managed to see Thimble. He looked terrible. He was thin, his fur was going all ways at once and his eyes, though they were still the colour of morning glory flowers, were sad and hurt.

The children sat round him and stroked him.

'I don't believe that Mrs Pim is nice to you,' said John.

'Does she feed you properly?' Judy asked.

Jennifer whispered, 'Is she rude to you? Your poor little face has an insulted look.'

After that, though often it was difficult, the children managed to see Thimble every day. Every day he looked worse. It was not that Mrs Pim was unkind to him; in fact she never spoke to him, for she despised cats. She did what she called 'her duty by him,' cooking his food every day and putting it out for him, but as far as possible she forgot he was in the house. Nor was it that he did not like the food Mrs Pim gave him because, in case he was hungry, the children brought him nice little snacks to tempt his appetite.

'But there must be something that makes him look so peculiar,' John said. 'If only you could talk, Thimble, and tell us what's the matter.'

Judy nearly cried.

'Your poor little face is so thin.'

Jennifer held him in her arms.

'He's lonely and he thinks nobody understands him any more; I can see it in his eyes.'

Just before Christmas, the children had a letter. It was written in pencil, in wobbly writing. It said: 'Coming home Christmas Day. Mrs Widgery.'

The children gazed at the letter in horror. Christmas Day! On Christmas Day Mrs Widgery would see Thimble. John faced facts.

'Seeing him will make her ill again.'

Judy moaned. 'She'll hardly know him, so thin as he is with such scratchy fur.'

Jennifer was staring out of the window. In her mind she was seeing Mrs Widgery coming home. She was seeing her opening her front door. She was seeing her sitting at her table. She could hear her scissors going snip, snap, and her voice saying, 'Let the pieces lie. Royal robes for a royal cat.' Suddenly, she bounded into the air.

'I know what's wrong with him. I know how we'll make him well by Christmas. Get your Christmas moneys, John and Judy. We're going shopping.'

On Christmas morning it was snowing hard.

Everything was muffled by the thick snow. Mrs Widgery got slowly out of a taxi. She tottered up to her front door. Using the wall and Mrs Pim's arm for support, she walked into the house. There was no sign it was Christmas day, for Mrs Pim did not hold with such nonsense as decorations. Mrs Widgery sank into a chair by her work-table. She called in a weak, thin voice, 'Thimble, Thimble.'

John, Judy and Jennifer, peeping in at the window, were waiting for just that. Very softly they opened the door and Thimble walked in.

Thimble looked splendid. On his head was a gold turban with a red feather in front. Round his neck was a collar which, if you did not look at it too closely, seemed to be made of emeralds, rubies and diamonds. On his tail was a big silver bow.

'What's this nonsense?' snapped Mrs Pim.

Mrs Widgery smiled happily.

'Bless you, Thimble. You look better than when I was taken ill. Somebody has known what my Thimble needs. Royal robes for a royal cat.'

The children looked at each other with shining eyes. They were glad the snow was so deep that Mrs

Widgery did not hear them creep away. They were so happy they held hands and danced up the street. As they danced, the Christmas bells began to peal. Other people might think that they rang: 'It's Christmas Day. It's Christmas Day.' But the children knew that what they were really singing was, 'Roy-al robes for a roy-al cat. Roy-al robes for a roy-al cat. It's Christ-mas Day it's Christ-mas Day. Roy-al robes for a roy-al cat.'

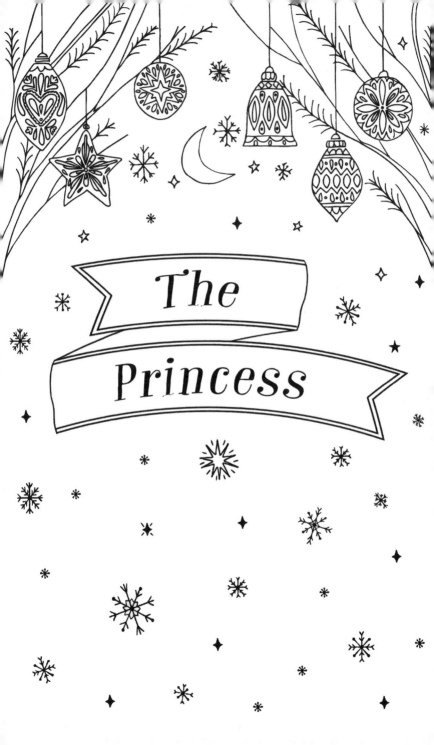

The Princess

Princess Stephanie knelt by the schoolroom fire and made toast. The palace, built of white marble, looked like a meringue, so the Princess's green-shuttered rooms on the top storey might have been a piece of angelica on the tip of the meringue. Far below, Stephanie could hear a string orchestra playing. She turned and grinned at Miss Stringer, her English governess.

'Poor Papa and Mama, the reception has started, all those terrible ambassadors and their wives in silly hats.'

Miss Stringer was a sandy, thin woman with kind, intelligent grey eyes. She had longed to live abroad, so had jumped at the chance when the father of a girl at the school where she was teaching had asked her if she would like to undertake the education of Princess Stephanie.

'I was attached to the Embassy there, got to know

the Royal Family well – I was sorry for the child. As you know, she is the only one and heir to the throne. Has had a pretty lonely time, I think. I imagine if you became her governess you might work on her parents to allow her to see more of children of her own age.'

Six weeks later Miss Stringer was installed in the Princess's suite, but though that was six months ago, she had not had success in finding friends for the child. She smiled at her now as she watched her making toast, but it was with a sigh at the back of her smile.

'They won't all be ambassadors, it's a big party.'

Stephanie gave a contented wriggle. 'So fortunate that you were able to get us out of going down. Before you came I always went to receptions dressed like a child in a picture book.'

Miss Stringer nodded. That was something she had done for Stephanie. 'A child of thirteen should not have her education interrupted by attending afternoon parties. You've made enough toast for six people.'

Stephanie brought the toast to the table. 'I'm glad you taught me about making toast. I never made any till you came.'

'Next time I'm out I will buy us some chestnuts

and you shall learn to roast them, as children do in England.'

Stephanie was a serious-looking child, her black hair fixed into tidy plaits wound round her head, and she had huge brown eyes. She leant towards Miss Stringer, her face alight with interest.

'Tell me more about English girls. How they go out alone to shop. How I would love to do that! Do you know, dear Miss Stringer, I have never in my whole life walked in the town.'

Miss Stringer knew only too well that Stephanie had never walked in the town; getting permission for her to do that was one of her plans.

'Perhaps tomorrow, if we go very early before the shop is properly open, I may be permitted to take you to shop in a store decorated for Christmas.'

Stephanie clasped her hands as if she were about to pray. 'Oh, Miss Stringer! Dear, dear Miss Stringer, if only that could happen!' Then her face fell. 'But I'm afraid Papa would never allow it. We've always sent one of Mama's ladies to do our shopping and I suppose we always will.'

'All the same, it may happen tomorrow, so I thought

after tea you might make out a list of everything you would like to buy.'

When the footman had cleared the tea table and made up the fire, Stephanie got out an exercise book, and in English, for she always had to talk and write in English except on Sundays, wrote in large letters 'Christmas presents'.

'I shall shop too,' said Miss Stringer. 'What would you like for Christmas?' She looked round the room, and thought of the equally well-equipped bedroom and dining-room. 'You seem to have everything.'

Stephanie eyed Miss Stringer thoughtfully. 'There is something I want more than anything in the world, but I don't think you'll give it to me because although no one's ever said so to me, it's something I'm not supposed to have.'

'What is it?'

Stephanie took a deep breath before she answered, so the words came out in a small explosion. 'Ballet shoes.'

Stephanie had dancing classes three times a week and was talented. Madame Arova, who taught her, was allowed to give her ballet training, but not on the pointes. 'It is not allowed, Princess,' Madame Arova had said sadly when Stephanie had asked if her feet were not now strong enough for blocked shoes. 'I understand your royal mother says a princess's feet are of national importance and must not be forced into unnatural positions. A pity, for were you a commoner, I could have made a dancer of you.'

Of course Miss Stringer knew all about Stephanie's dancing.

'I oughtn't to give them to you,' she said weakly, 'but I've never been told you weren't to have them so . . . '

Stephanie jumped out of her chair and flung her arms round Miss Stringer's neck. 'Darling, darling Miss Stringer! Pink satin with proper satin ribbons?'

Miss Stringer laughed. 'If – and mind you it's still if – I give you ballet shoes, it's you who will have to choose them. Imagine me trying on ballet shoes!'

They were still laughing at the ridiculous picture of Miss Stringer in ballet shoes when the footman came in. He bowed to Stephanie.

'The guests are leaving, Your Royal Highness.'

Stephanie waited until he had gone out, then she got up and rang the bell for her maid. 'I'd better get changed and so had you. Oh, wouldn't it be gorgeous if Mama gives permission for me to do my own shopping!'

Though often Miss Stringer had doubted it, she was considered a success as Stephanie's governess. She had always been open to new ideas, so it did not distress her as it would have done some teachers to have to adapt her teaching methods to Stephanie's needs. A princess, she was told, must be able to stand without moving or appearing tired for hours on end. So Stephanie did all her oral work standing. A princess must be able to recognise an acquaintance immediately and know their name. From Queen Victoria of England's training, Miss Stringer stole the use of dolls. Each new person Stephanie met had a doll model whom Stephanie, without warning, had to recognise and name. A princess must always make a good entrance. Miss Stringer was used to schoolgirls tumbling into her classes, but she was stern with Stephanie, making her come into her classroom and dining-room as if she were coming into a vast hall where thousands were waiting to see her. To help Stephanie, Miss Stringer, who was no actress, would sometimes on their walks in the Palace grounds turn herself into a cheering crowd to whom

Stephanie had to smile and give the curious little flicking gesture of the hand which was the royal wave.

Since also Miss Stringer was a brilliant teacher, it did not pass unnoticed how Stephanie was in every way coming on, so Stephanie's parents had decided to trust Miss Stringer's judgement and allow the great treat of a personal shopping expedition.

When Stephanie, beautifully dressed, came in to them followed by Miss Stringer, the King said, 'Miss Stringer believes it would be of use to you to come in contact with my people. So Mama and I have decided that tomorrow you may shop at Fouquier's store.'

'I have never done such a thing myself,' said the Queen, 'but I believe you must handle money. Is that so, Miss Stringer?'

'Usually,' Miss Stringer agreed. 'On this occasion I or the Princess's detective could, but I think it would be of value to the Princess to use her own purse.'

The King nodded agreement. 'Very well, you may ... You will, of course, be incognito save for the manager of the store who, naturally, knows you are coming; you have not been seen in public often so it is unlikely you will be recognised.'

Stephanie was so excited at the thought of tomorrow that she could scarcely get her words out. 'Oh Papa! Thank you, Papa. Thank you, Mama.'

The next morning a car without the royal coat of arms drove up to Fouquier's store and Stephanie stepped out. It was true the manager was on the doorstep to greet her, but following instructions he merely gave a quick bow and she was inside the shop. It was the most exciting experience. It was not only that the store glittered with Christmas decorations, but nobody knew her, so suddenly she was just an ordinary girl of thirteen. She knew this and loved knowing it, and when a boy about her own age shoved her to one side as he charged towards the lift and model engines, she said, her eyes blazing like stars, 'He pushed me, just as if I was anybody. Oh, Miss Stringer, it's such fun being pushed.'

They did the serious shopping first. All the things on Stephanie's list and some on Miss Stringer's, and everywhere Stephanie paid for what she had bought, and often had to wait to pay, standing in a queue.

'I'm like Alice in Wonderland,' she told Miss Stringer. 'This morning I was me, a Princess, and now I'm nobody. That woman when I paid her said: "Come along, dreamer. We haven't all day to wait." Imagine me having that said to me! Goodness, I am enjoying myself!'

The ballet shoes were sold at the end of the ordinary shoe shop. On the wall was a big notice: 'Special children's performance in the theatre at 11 am and 3 pm.'

'When we've bought the shoes could we go and see that?' Stephanie begged. 'It's ten minutes to eleven.'

Stephanie's excitement and the gay Christmas atmosphere had gone to Miss Stringer's head.

'I'm sure you can. I'll ask if we need tickets.' She turned to the detective. 'Do you know where tickets are procured?' Together they moved towards a shop assistant.

A very young salesgirl fitted Stephanie into the perfect size ballet shoes.

'Are you dancing in the show today?'

Stephanie was so proud at being taken for a professional dancer that she could only smile, and she smiled more when, just to try them out, she raised herself on to her pointes.

73

'Oh look,' she breathed to herself in the mirror, 'that's you in real, proper ballet shoes.'

The shoes set her dreaming, but she came back to the shop when she felt her arm shaken. She looked round to find a boy of about her own age standing beside her.

'Do come on, I guessed it was you. We'll have to hurry, the show begins at eleven.' And without waiting for her to answer, and before the young shop assistant had time to stop her, he had pulled her out of the room and into the elevator.

'You've made a mistake,' said Stephanie. 'Who did you think I was?'

'You're Carola,' said the boy. 'The girl they've sent to dance with me instead of Bettina – she's got chicken-pox. An awful nuisance. I hate dancing with a strange partner.'

Nice as it was to be unknown for a change, this was too much.

'You don't like a strange partner! What about me?'

'You!' said the boy. 'Why, you're nobody. You've never danced in public until today, they told me that. Me, I'm well known.'

Never danced in public until today! That made Stephanie think.

'What were you and Bettina going to dance?'

The boy looked despisingly at her. 'Do you think I don't know you've been practising the mazurka ever since you knew yesterday you were going to dance it?'

Now the mazurka was a national dance which Stephanie had danced since she was small, but there was a ballet version, and this she had recently learnt. What fun, what superb fun just once not to dance alone but to dance properly in front of a real live audience with a real boy!

The elevator stopped and she seized the boy's hand. 'Come on, let's run.'

Downstairs, the shoe department was being turned upside down. The manager of the store arrived looking green and wringing his hands. The head buyer and the head saleswoman were told the awful truth and nearly fainted. The detective lined up everybody in the shoe shop and asked questions. Only Miss Stringer remained calm.

'There's a simple explanation,' she said over and over again. 'Somebody will know where she is.'

The young salesgirl who had been looking after Stephanie was standing cold with horror, holding Stephanie's shoes. At home there were five brothers and sisters, all of whom were hoping for more to eat because she had got herself a job in the shoe department of Fouquier's. And now, when she had only worked there one week, she had committed the unforgivable crime – she had let a client go without paying. Tears rolled down her cheeks.

Miss Stringer did not know what made her turn round to look at the salesgirl, but when she did she was across the shop and by her side in a minute.

'Where did you get those shoes?'

'They were the client's,' sobbed the girl. 'Such a nice young lady she seemed, I never thought she'd run off like that. I hardly saw them go and by the time I did they were in the elevator.'

'Them!' said Miss Stringer, scared for the first time as masked assassins chased before her eyes. 'Them!'

'Yes, her and the boy ... He fetched her like.'

Miss Stringer looked at the shoes. 'Did she go with bare feet?'

This brought on a fresh flood of tears.

'She was wearing the ballet shoes and she never paid. Oh, what will I do?'

Miss Stringer left the crying girl and joined the detective.

'The Princess ran off with a boy. She was wearing ballet shoes. It seems she ran, she was not forced. Do you think ... ?'

The manager, still looking green, drew near. 'Any news of Her Highness?'

The detective looked at Miss Stringer. 'You think she's run up to see the show? Well, no harm having a look.'

He hurried towards the elevator and Miss Stringer ran beside him. The manager followed them and the buyer and the head saleswoman followed him, and behind them, still carrying Stephanie's shoes and still crying, came the little salesgirl.

'Up to the theatre,' said the manager to the elevator operator, 'And don't stop for no one.'

The boy and Stephanie were dancing the mazurka. It was the ballet version Stephanie had learnt and was showy technically. The children and their parents in the audience were enthralled and stamped their feet and clapped their hands in time to the music. But it was not only the music and dancing that delighted them, it was Stephanie. With every step she danced she threw off more and more of the stifling etiquette which had swaddled her since she was a baby. Her left foot kicked away detectives. Her right foot dismissed all ladies-in-waiting. As she leapt in the air, she left Princess Stephanie behind and came down

just Stephanie from anywhere. Oh, it was glorious, glorious! Never had she been so happy.

'Who on earth is she?' the dancing mistress asked. 'She's not a bit like that dumb Carola, and anyway we know she too has started chicken-pox.'

The mazurka came to an end and breathlessly the boy bowed while Stephanie curtsied.

'I say,' the boy said, 'you are good. You'll go places. Come on, give them one more bow.'

Stephanie moved to give a lovely, sweeping theatrical curtsey. Then she stopped, gasped, and ran off the stage.

'Why did you do that?' asked the boy. 'It was jolly rude.'

Stephanie was tearing off her stage costume. 'I can't explain. If we meet again – and perhaps we will some day – I might be able to.'

Miss Stringer, holding Stephanie's hand, led her to the car. The detective got in front with the chauffeur.

'There's the manager, dear,' said Miss Stringer.

Stephanie gave her Princess smile and a fluttering wave of the hand.

Just before they reached the palace, Miss Stringer

said, 'Don't worry, dear. You were not recognised, no one will know.'

Stephanie turned a glowing face to her.

'I'm not worrying and if everybody knew I wouldn't mind.' She watched the sentries present arms and heard the gates crash together behind the car.

Then she patted the box on her knee. 'Thank goodness I've got my ballet shoes. They'll help me to remember.'

The
Chain

David and his father and mother got miserably out of the car. Mother said, 'I'll get tea.' Then she shut the kitchen door.

Father, speaking in a growly voice, said that this was as good a moment as any to put a new washer on the bathroom tap. Then he shut the bathroom door.

David looked at the two shut doors, and went into the sitting-room. Then he slammed the sitting-room door. If everybody were going to shut themselves up, he would shut himself up too.

There was a gorgeous fire. David sat on the rug and looked at it. If only Judith had got well and had come home in time for Christmas! It was queer, but he had never guessed how much Judith being there mattered until she went to hospital. After all, he was eleven and she was only nine, and he would not have thought a girl of that age would have been much use, but Christmas was not Christmas without her. If she had been home, they would be roasting chestnuts on that fire. What was the fun of decorating the house alone? It wasn't much good hanging up a stocking when you were only one. How dull, opening a stocking by himself, without Judith squeaking, 'Ooh! Look, David! Look what I've got!'

David lay down on the mat. He tried to read his book. It was *Treasure Island*, but even *Treasure Island* was not the book it usually was. It was so stupid Judith was not home. Up until today everybody had thought she would be. 'She must get out of bed by herself and be able to walk round the ward,' the doctor said, 'then she can go home.' But in spite of knowing this, Judith had not got out of bed. Every day she had tried, and every day she had failed. 'It isn't me who can't walk,' she had explained. 'Inside me I'm not just walking, I'm running, but when I try to do it my legs go wobbly and fall me over.'

Crossly, David flicked over a page and found himself looking at a picture of Long John Silver. He poked with his finger at the arm that held the crutch. 'If you were real, I bet you'd get her up. I can just hear you saying, "Can't get out of bed says you? Then you aren't trying says I. Split my sides, I've a sick heart when I look at the likes of you."'

Staring at the picture of Long John, David could almost imagine him alive. 'Then you'd start doing something. Being you, you wouldn't do it yourself, you'd be the one to shout the orders and make other people do it for you. I know what you'd do. You'd get other people out of books, especially the ones Judith likes best, to make a sort of chain, and they'd pull, and they'd pull, until she was out of bed, and simply tearing round the ward.'

He knelt up so that he could read the titles of his and Judith's books in the shelves. They went back to the days when they had been very little. He leant down again so that he could speak to the picture of Long John. 'Almost I can see the chain. The little ones are in front. There's Peter Rabbit and Mrs Tiggy-Winkle and Orlando, he won't be much help but he'll come and pull, and the *Just So* animals, and Pooh, goodness I'd forgotten you Pooh, and Simpkin and the mice. Then behind them there's

Alice and the White Rabbit and all those, and
Moley and Ratty, and of course Toad. I bet Toad is
sick at having to help pull. He's the sort who wants
to direct operations like you. Then as it's for Judith
there are her special ones, Peter Pan – he won't be
much help, he'll just stooge around – and those
four girls out of *Little Women*. And that girl Velvet
that rode the Grand National winner, I bet she's a
good puller. And Nancy Blackett and those others
in the Ransome books. You'll like them John, first-
rate seamen like you said Cap'n Smollett was. Black
Beauty's there, he's tired, poor old fellow, but he's
still got some pull left in him. Oh, and Robinson
Crusoe and Man Friday, and David Copperfield, and
Captain Ahab – I wish he could have brought Moby
Dick – and that gorgeous bear that read *The Times*
in *The Wind on the Moon*. As Judith likes them we'd
better have those beastly Water Babies and that hor-
rible Mary from *The Secret Garden*. And of course
Kim. Oh, and masses and masses of Red Indians all
in their war paint.'

David was so carried away by the chain he was
inventing that suddenly it ceased to be an invention

and became real. He stopped thinking who ought to be part of the chain and just saw books open and all kinds of creatures hop out. Many of them he had forgotten, lots he was not sure he had ever known. The room was crowded. Animals, children, ballet dancers, clowns, old men and old women, fathers and mothers, fairies, pirates, and kings, queens, jesters, courtiers, and, arriving with an awful bump, a big weight for the end of the chain, an old friend David had not seen for years, Babar. Long John was in the middle of them all, his parrot screeching oaths, while he waved his crutch – 'Come on, you land-lubbers, shiver my timbers, dooty is dooty, messmates. Dash my buttons, come on all of you.'

As his shout rang round the room, the radio set opened, and out tumbled a crowd jostling, laughing; not all good pullers, but nearly all with stout hearts. Worzel Gummidge, pushing forward firmly, followed by Earthy carefully shepherding Scairy. Tammy Troot all the way from Scotland. Biffer roaring into the room, barking his head off, telling Long John to put him in the toughest place where the most pulling was needed. Brilliantly efficient and on the spot, Norman and Henry Bones, rolling up their sleeves as they ran to help, and behind them, panting a little because they had come a long way, Bill with Storm barking to him to hurry. Mr Mayor telling Long John pompously that in spite of his position he was willing to help. The Magician wanting to invent a chain which would save anybody having to pull anything, Larry and Dennis struggling to push past Mr Mayor without seeming rude. Last of all Jennings. He rushed up to Long John. 'I say, sir, there's somebody here David and Judith don't know. You see, sir, they haven't got a television set, but he so wanted to help I've brought him along.'

David leant forward to see who it was that Jennings had brought. Before he could see, a roar from Long John told him. 'Shiver my timbers, it's Muffin. Into your place, my hearty. Wait till I give the word to pull, I'll give it soon, you can lay to that my son.'

In an instant the word was given.

'Pull!' roared Long John.

'Pull!' squeaked, grunted, and cried a million little voices, 'Pull!' David shouted, 'Pull! Pull! Pull!'

※

The door opened. Mother switched on the light.

'Who's pulling, darling? I could hear you shouting right out in the kitchen.'

David blinked. He looked round the empty room. 'I was pretending. I thought how gorgeous it would be if Long John came out of this book and got everybody in the other books to help him to make a chain to pull Judith out of bed. You know, after a bit I stopped pretending and it felt as if it really happened, and not only out of books, but out of the air. You should have seen the help that came from the Children's Hour. Everybody pulled marvellously. It was like magic.'

Mother looked at him in an odd sort of way. 'It was magic. Didn't you hear the telephone? It was the hospital. Five minutes ago, Judith got out of bed as easily as if she hadn't been ill, and walked round the ward. Daddy has gone in the car to fetch her home.'

Christmas at Collers

Only two weeks to Christmas. The children came rushing home from school, bursting with news. They found their mother in her bedroom.

'Mum,' said George, the eldest, who was fourteen, 'If it doesn't rain, will you come and see the Regent Street decorations on Saturday? Everybody says they're terrific this year.'

Pauline, who was twelve, looked up at her mother with shining eyes. 'It's so gay out today, Mum. The sun shining on the shop Christmas trees makes them look as if it was real frost.'

'And there's simply thousands of people shopping,' Alistair, who was ten, added. 'Heaps of them come to London just to look. Lucky us to live here.'

Sandra, the baby of the family, was eight. She was so excited her feet danced while she tried to make herself heard. 'Mum! Mum! Mum! I've been asked to two more parties, that's six already and . . . '

The children's mother had been kneeling on the floor, packing what her family supposed was a Christmas present. Now she got up and they saw it was not a present she was packing, but her own clothes. She was a person who hated beating about the bush.

'I'm sorry, George, Regent Street is out this year, and so are your parties, Sandra. We're going away.'

'Going away!' Eight astonished eyes looked up at her. The children had been born in their London home and had only left it for a fortnight each summer. Their house, to other people, might look part of a grimy, ordinary Hammersmith road, but the children never thought of it in that way – it was home.

'Going where?' Pauline asked.

Their mother sat down on her bed and patted it to invite the children to sit, too. Pauline and Alistair sat beside her, George and Sandra faced them on their father's bed.

'It's Granny. As you know, she's been alone since Grandfather died, and now she's had a fall.'

Of course the children knew about Granny. They had never seen her, for she and Grandfather only had a cottage without room in it for grandchildren, but they received little presents for birthdays and Christmas, and at Christmas sent small gifts in return, usually made by themselves. When Grandfather had died, they were sorry because their mother was sad and because she went away for the funeral. But what happened to Granny and Grandfather was like something happening to people in a book; it was quite different from what happened to Dadsmum and Dadsdad. They lived in London, and at least once in each month either came to tea in Hammersmith or invited the family to tea in St John's Wood with them.

It was thinking of Dadsmum and Dadsdad that first pulled George out of the sort of daze his mother's news had thrown him into. 'But what about Dadsdad and Dadsmum? Where will they eat their turkey and plum pudding if they don't come here?'

'Yes, where?' the others chimed in.

Their mother made a sympathetic face. 'I've thought of that. But they'll understand. They've had us every year and they've got each other, but Granny's all alone, in a very lonely place.'

It was when their mother said those last words that the full awfulness of what was to happen to them hit the children. They had heard a lot about Colerton, locally called Collers, where their mother had lived when she was a child. It was near Exmoor. Collers had been quite a village, but now people had moved away and there were only about ten inhabited cottages left, of which Granny's was one. There were not even enough people in Collers now for a rector to give all his time to, so except for summer visitors, the rectory was empty, for Collers shared a rector with another parish. The children's father, who was as completely a Londoner as they were, had christened Collers 'Collers-on-the-mud' and had often made them laugh describing how, when he was engaged to their mother, the woman in the only shop had said to him, 'Oh my dear soul, you'll be the foreigner that's marrying our Anne.' And now even today he was probably still called by everybody, 'Our Anne's foreigner.'

Pauline did not mean to sound angry, but she did.

'Not Christmas, Mum! If Granny wants to see you, see her after the holidays. She couldn't want us to miss the pantomime, the parties and ... well, just all Christmas.'

'Of course she couldn't,' the other three chimed in.

Their mother looked despairing. 'Miss all Christmas indeed! What dreadfully town children I've got. To tell you the truth, I've never thought Christmas in London was proper Christmas. Anyway, we're going, so the sooner you make up your minds to it, the better.'

The children looked as disgusted as they felt.

'When?' Alistair asked.

'The day after school breaks up.'

'We can't go then,' George said, 'Dad'll still be working.'

'I know that,' his mother agreed. 'But he'll be with us on Christmas Eve.'

'Poor Dad!' Sandra looked reproachfully at her mother. 'I bet he's mad at having to go.'

'He took the news much better than you children have. I told him on the telephone after I got Granny's letter, and he said he quite understood.'

Pauline knew she was behaving badly, but she could not stop herself. 'You haven't told us yet why we have to go.'

'I did. Granny has had a fall, she's strained a muscle and can't get around. She's been in hospital but she'll be home next week. We can't have her hobbling about alone, can we?'

As far as the children were concerned, their unknown Granny was welcome to hobble alone, but seeing as she was their mother's mother, they could not say that.

'Where are we going to sleep?' George asked. 'You said there were only two bedrooms, which is why we've never stayed.'

Their mother smiled, hoping at last she had something to tell them which would please them.

'You are being lent the rectory. You'll eat in Granny's cottage, but for the rest of the time you'll be on your own. Don't you think that will be rather fun?'

Fun! The children could hardly believe what they had heard. Their house, number 31, was joined to 29 on one side and 33 on the other, so if for a short while one of them was in alone, it was not like being alone, for the noises of the Smiths in 29 and the Browns in 33 were so clear it was as if they were in the house. Every summer, for two enchanted weeks in August, the whole family went to a camp on the Kent coast. There they had their chalets, the girls in one, the boys in another, and father and mother in a third. But though the chalets were not attached to their neighbours as was their house in Hammersmith, nothing could be more joined up than chalet life, for you ate, bathed, played and went in for competitions with the other campers, so you were never alone for a second. On their own! Sleeping by themselves! No father and mother within call! It might be all right in summer in a nice place with plenty to do, but not at Christmas in Collers.

'Have you ever stayed in the rectory, Mum?' Pauline asked.

'Perhaps there's a telephone,' Alistair suggested, 'so we can ring you up if we want you.'

Sandra was fond of her food. 'I suppose there'll be things to eat in it. I mean, in case we're hungry in the middle of the night.'

Their mother felt she must have brought up her

children badly. 'Oh dear, and I thought you'd be pleased. You must wait to find out the answers. It's years since I was in the rectory. As a small girl it seemed enormous to me after our cottage, but I don't suppose it is really. I certainly never stayed there. There was a big hall, I remember, where there were Christmas parties. There won't be a telephone, Alistair, I think nobody has the telephone in Collers. They use the telephone box. I can't have you starving, Sandra, so I'll put in some cocoa and biscuits, but George and Pauline will be in charge of them.'

Their mother seemed so certain the children ought to find living alone in a rectory fun that even Sandra did not say what they were all thinking – which was that it sounded uncomfortable, if not frightening. But while their mother was cooking supper, and they were laying the table, they spoke their minds.

'It's a shame we have to go,' said Pauline. 'Think of everything we'll miss.'

'I bet there's nothing to do,' George growled.

Alistair heard their father come in and went into the hall to meet him. 'It's awful, isn't it, Dad?' he whispered.

His father followed him into the living-room. 'To town chaps like me and you, yes, but your mother thinks Collers the finest place on earth, so we must make the best of it.'

Pauline tucked an arm into one of his. 'Why can't Granny come here for Christmas? She could be pushed in one of those station chairs up the platform, couldn't she?'

Her father pulled her ponytail. 'Just out of hospital! What an idea!'

'Well, an ambulance, then,' George suggested.

The children's father was seldom angry with them, but this time he was.

'Ambulance, nothing! You're a selfish lot. It won't hurt you to have your Christmas upset for one year. Now there's no grumbling. You're going to Collers and whatever you feel, for Mum's sake you're going to pretend you like it.'

❄

Pretending to like going to Collers was not helped by it being a most exhausting journey to get there. First there was a train to Barnstable. Then after that, a long wait for a slow train to the junction. There a taxi waiting to take them to Collers.

'We'll go straight to the rectory,' their mother told the driver. 'Bed's the place for my family, they're half asleep already.'

The driver started his car.

'You're right there, me dear, and the old lady will like to have you to herself. She's beside herself, me dear soul, that you're coming.'

Arrangements had been made for someone to get the rectory ready, so a log fire was burning in the grate in the hall, the beds were made up and aired, and there was a big jug of milk, a crusty loaf, half a pound of butter and a dozen eggs in the larder. But that night the children scarcely took in their surroundings, not even that they had supper by lamplight and went to bed with candles. The next morning, however, they saw everything and were appalled.

George was awake first and, pulling on his dressing-gown, made a quick, teeth-chattering tour of inspection. Pauline heard him going back to the room he shared with Alistair, and called out to him.

'What's it like?'

Shivering, George came into the girls' room and sat on Pauline's bed. 'Ghastly. Do you know, there's only cold water?'

'We washed in hot last night,' said Sandra, stretching and yawning.

George sounded as gloomy as he felt. 'Boiled in a kettle on a gas stove which has the gas in a great jar thing. I mean it isn't laid on like ordinary gas.'

Pauline pointed to her candle. 'Imagine, no electric light.'

'What!' Alistair, who had just opened the door, gave a horrified howl. 'Then there's no telly. What do we do in the evenings without a telly?'

Pauline got out of bed and put on her dressing-gown. She gave an imitation of their father. 'There's to be no grumbling.' Then she added, 'Go and light the gas for the kettle, George, I'm starving and we must wash before we meet Granny.'

Alistair thought that unnecessary. 'Not me. I bet she won't notice.'

But Granny did notice. Though only just out of hospital, she was dressed and sitting in a chair when her grandchildren arrived and were introduced to her. As their mother said who each was, she looked up at them with eyes that missed nothing.

'Aren't you old enough to wash yourself, grandson?' she said to Alistair. 'That face has not been washed this morning and neither have those teeth.'

Pauline, though she thought Alistair ought to have washed, was not having him bullied by a strange grandmother. 'We had to wait for the kettle to boil on the gas, and one kettle's not much for four people.'

Grandmother had a face as wrinkled as a last season's walnut, but now it was wrinkled more than ever with a sort of sad scorn.

'Do your children have to wash in hot water, Anne? You used cold and often broke the ice.' Then she turned to Pauline. 'Don't waste gas, child. If you must have hot water, keep a good fire of logs going in the rectory hall and stand a full kettle on it, that way you've hot water whenever you need it.'

One thing about Collers which none of the children could complain about was the food. There was a splendid breakfast, which included new bread, a big bowl of clotted cream and bilberry jelly. But even the best breakfast can't last for ever and presently the children got up, thinking gloomily of the cold rectory and unmade beds.

'Are you coming with us, Mum?' Sandra asked hopefully.

But it was Grandmother who answered. 'She is not. Your mother has more than enough to do here. Now run along, all of you, tidy the rectory, there's logs for the fire in the shed, then you can take a look round until dinner at one o'clock.'

It was a beastly day, cold, blowy and, though not exactly raining, there was a dampish mist which Grandmother called a 'missel'. It was not the sort of day the children would dream of going out, unless it was to the cinema or something like that. Grumpily they made the beds, unpacked and, with the aid of a whole candle, succeeded in lighting the hall fire.

'I feel like a castaway,' said Alistair.

'But castaways,' Sandra pointed out, 'hope for ships to come. We know there won't be one.'

Pauline pulled a table up to the fire. 'Get the car racing game, George. Thank goodness we packed it.'

And that is what the children did between meals for the next three days. It was odd, but they were asked no questions. Perhaps Granny and their mother had too much to talk about to be interested, but there was a look in Grandmother's eyes when she remarked, 'No second helpings? Running about in the country you ought to be starved,' that made them uncomfortable. Could she possibly guess that they spent all their time playing games in front of a hot fire?

Then, on the fourth day, the wood ran out. Alistair, whose turn it was to go to the shed, came back with only three logs. 'I've looked everywhere and that's all there is.'

Sandra helped him arrange the logs in the fireplace. 'Granny will know where there's a shop where you can buy them.'

George and Pauline exchanged looks which meant, 'Oh, don't let's ask Granny, she'll think us fools.'

Out loud, George said, 'It's not raining. Let's go down the street. Someone will know who sells logs.'

It was a cold morning, so after breakfast, wrapped up in everything they possessed, the children went down the village street. Nobody seemed to be about, so they decided to knock on one of the cottage doors. It was opened by a young woman with a baby in her arms. She greeted them with a warm smile.

'Good morning, my dear souls, so you've come out at last, have you? We've been wondering when you'd be around. "Funny," we said, "there's Granny Sales's grandchildren up to the rectory and never sight nor sound of 'em.""

Pauline felt it was best to come to the point. 'Could you tell us where there's a place that sells logs? We've finished all the ones at the rectory.'

The woman laughed. 'There's no shop in Collers now, mostly we shop at the Moor Junction, but not for logs, my dear souls, no.'

'Then how do logs come?' Alistair asked.

The woman laughed again. 'It's plain you're from London. There's lots of wood to be had for the pickin' up left by the tree fellers.'

'Where?' George asked.

The woman pointed. 'Follow down there, that will bring you to the place where you'll find the children have gone to cut the Christmas tree for the church and to pick holly.'

The children of Collers, eight of them of all ages, were coming home, pulling a Christmas tree on a sort of sledge, and carrying sacks of holly and evergreens when the family met them. Everybody grinned at everybody else.

'I say,' said George to the oldest-looking of the Collers boys, 'We've run out of wood for the fire. Could you show us where there's some we can pick up?'

The boy looked at their empty hands. 'What're you carrying it in?'

'You've got no sack,' a girl pointed out.

But they were friendly children, so they turned their holly and evergreens out on to the ground and left the tree and the sledge and led the way back to an open space where trees had been felled. Sure enough, lying about was wood for a hundred fires. It was, of course, impossible to use other people's sacks to fetch your wood and not offer to go back afterwards to help pick up the spilled holly and evergreens. Besides, the children wanted to. For the first time since they had come to Collers, they had enjoyed their morning.

For the first time, too, the children came into dinner

ragingly hungry. They would have supposed Granny
and their mother, walled in though they were by the
old days about which they were always talking, would
have noticed when Alistair had a third helping of
potatoes, but they did not seem to. But there was a
different tone in Granny's voice when she said, as she
always did after dinner, 'Run along, Grandchildren, I
am sure you have lots to do.'

'It's as if Granny was expecting something from us,'
Pauline said. 'I wouldn't mind if it was only her. But

you would think Mum would be more interested. She never asks where we go or what we do.'

'Just as well until today,' George pointed out, 'for we went nowhere and did nothing.'

✳

The next morning, even before the beds were made, the children of Collers were knocking on the rectory door.

'You'd better hurry, we're making church decorations this morning.'

'Make!' said Sandra. 'Us? We don't know how to.'

A small girl grinned at her. 'We'll show you how.'

The eldest boy nodded. 'Sure enough. It's garlands we're making today for the hanging tomorrow.'

'While we make, we sing,' a red-headed girl explained.

George looked as puzzled as he felt. 'Sing what?'

The red-headed girl laughed. 'Oh, my dear souls, you've a lot to learn. Tis for the New Year's wassailing.'

Making garlands, though the Collers children thought nothing of it, was a skilled business. The smallest cut up the evergreens and holly while their elders bound the pieces on to fine ropes, for in Collers church it was traditional that ropes of greenery were looped between pillar and pillar. The family, except for Pauline, accepted that garland-making was not for them and joined the cutters up.

Presently it was time for singing. The children were taught the words, which began, 'Wassail, wassail all over the town! The cup is white and the ale is brown,' and a chorus which went, 'For it's your wassail and our wassail. And it's joy be to you, and a jolly wassail.'

'Not very church music,' Sandra whispered to Alistair, who agreed with her but was too busy singing to say so.

The next day the church was decorated in the morning, and in the afternoon everybody got sledges out from where they had lain all the summer. They needed oiling, and some of them a coat of paint, and the children helped.

'Oh, my dear soul, you wait to the New Year. Snow falls so thick hereabouts, Collers is buried for a week at a time.'

It was during the oiling of the sledges that the family knew there was a secret. There were nods and whispers and looks. Then at last they were told. Each Christmas Eve in Collers there took place what was called The Carolling.

'It's been goin' on I dunno how many years,' the Collers children said.

One of the girls – this year it was red-headed Polly – was dressed as the Virgin and rode on an ass through the village, escorted by the eldest boy in Collers, dressed as Joseph. At each cottage, they knocked and cried, 'We be poor wayfarers, let us in, let us in.' But no one answered. At the end of the street, the rest of the Collers children were waiting, wearing animal masks and capes, and they led Mary and Joseph to a newly painted barn. There, while waiting for Joseph to announce the birth of Jesus, they processed round the barn, singing carols. Once, there had been every kind of beast and bird waiting to escort Mary and Joseph to the barn, but since people had moved away from the village, only a sheep, horse, cow, raven, dove and a goat were present. No one ever talked fast in Collers, so this took time to explain, but in the end the children understood that they were to be among the waiting animals.

It seemed the dressing-up clothes lived in the vestry, and sure enough there was an old box, and out of it came a dog's mask and cloak for George, a cat's mask for Pauline, a rabbit's for Alistair and a robin's for Sandra.

'Oh, I do like being a robin,' said Sandra. 'And when we've finished carolling, do we go in the barn and see the baby?'

'Look now,' the eldest boy explained, 'you go in and kneel but there's a lot more carolling, for that's when our folks come.'

Bit by bit, the children picked up what happened. Once, and old people could remember it, food and drink was what the grown-ups brought, and there was a kind of party, but now it was parcels for an old people's home.

※

Of course, the carols for the carolling needed rehearsing, and so did the family's part in the animal procession, and there were two hilarious bus journeys to the shops, for if you make eight new friends, they need cards and Christmas presents. With one thing and another, the days rushed by, and suddenly Christmas Eve was one day away.

Pauline and George were building the fire when Pauline said, 'We ought to tell Mum everything. I mean about us being animals tomorrow and the wassailing on New Year's Day – well, everything. I mean, she most likely thinks we still hate being here.'

George sat up on his haunches. 'It's so difficult to start. I mean, we made all that fuss about coming, you can't just say out of the blue, "It's jolly decent in Collers".'

Pauline lit the fire. 'Actually, it's the nicest Christmas we've ever had.'

Alistair had come down the stairs and heard what they were saying. 'It's Granny. She never asks us things, so when can we say we didn't want to come but now we like it?'

'It's Dad I'm fussed about,' George explained. 'We ought to have written, really. Suppose he's been thinking all this time we're hating it and has planned to take us home with him on Sunday.'

Sandra had joined them. 'He couldn't do that. No wassailing, no tobogganing, just dirty old London.'

'I wish we'd written,' said George. 'We look sort of silly liking it here after making such a fuss.'

Pauline was staring at the fire. 'We ought really to ask Mum and Dad to the carolling tomorrow.'

George thought of himself kneeling by the crib, wearing a dog's head. 'We can't. They'd laugh, and anyway, Mum couldn't leave Granny, and Dad will only just have arrived.'

Pauline was not convinced. 'I think we ought just to ask them. They can say no, but otherwise Dad will wonder where we are on his first evening.'

But somehow the asking never happened. Granny's brisk, twinkling-eyed manner put them off.

'I feel if I told her,' George admitted, 'she would say, "Of course, Grandson. What else would you be on Christmas Eve except a dog?"'

Pauline giggled. 'I know just what you mean, but it seems unfair that Dad and Mum will be the only grown-ups who aren't there.'

❄

Dad arrived in time for a late lunch, and afterwards settled down in a chair for a sleep. Their mother was cooking and wanted no help, and Granny, sitting in her chair, was busy sewing and with her thoughts, so it was easy for the children to slip away.

It was dark when the clip-clop of the donkey's feet told the waiting animals that Mary and Joseph had left the village and were on their way to the barn.

'One. Two. Three,' said the choir leader. The children took deep breaths.

> *Tyrley, tyrlow, tyrley, tyrlow,*
> *So merrily the shepherds began to blow*

The smallest children led the donkey, so Sandra had a hand on his bridle and though she knew it was Polly on his back, it looked like Mary, so Sandra felt part of Christmas.

The animals left Mary and Joseph in the barn while they marched round outside keeping watch and singing. When they came into the barn, there in the manger was a baby. It was a figure used so long, it was perhaps old and even a little soiled, but none of the animals noticed it. They knelt in a circle, horse and cow on either side of Joseph, the little goat and the robin at the foot of the manger stall, and they sang 'Once in Royal David's City'.

Then the door creaked open and in came the first grown-ups, looking as surprised at what they saw as if the men had not rigged up lights and painted the barn. Each carried a parcel which they held out to the baby before laying it on the ground. 'I wish,' thought Pauline, 'we'd told Mum and Dad. It was mean of us. After all, other people make mistakes. We were silly, that was all.'

The grown-ups came slowly, two by two, singing as they came, and as each laid down a parcel, they moved into the shadows in the corners of the barn. Then, when the last of the villagers had come, the door was opened wide and there was the children's mother singing with the best, making room for Granny's wheelchair, which their father was pushing. 'And each of them,' as Sandra said afterwards, 'brought a parcel.'

'And why wouldn't we, Granddaughter?' Granny laughed. 'Why, your mother was Mary one year, and I was a fox from the time I was six.'

Granny was much more approachable that evening.

'You never asked if we were being animals.'

Granny's eyes twinkled. 'Those who come looking sour need time to find their way. "Leave them be," I said to your mother. "Leave them be."'

Their father looked from child to child. 'Who'd like to come back to London with me on Sunday? I'm willing to take you.'

They flung themselves on him.

'Silly Dad!'

'It's marvellous. The nicest Christmas we ever had.'

Their father raised an eyebrow. 'Hear that, Anne? You said Collers would get them, and it seems it has.'

The Pantomime Goose

The Bandler family lived in London, but the Bandler children had spent every Christmas of their lives in different towns. Their father, Bert Bandler, was a comedian most of the year, but at Christmas he acted in pantomime as a goose. Bert was a very good goose and so, whenever a manager was putting on *Mother Goose*, one of the first orders he gave was, 'Engage Bert Bandler.'

This Christmas it had looked as if everything was going wrong. No manager wrote to engage Bert.

'I can't understand it,' Bert said to Mrs Bandler, whose name was Effie. ''Tisn't natural.' He turned over his theatrical paper and tapped the advertisements. '*Cinderella, Jack and the Beanstalk, Sleeping Beauty, Puss in Boots, Puss in Boots, Puss in Boots*. Proper epidemic of *Puss in Boots* and not one *Mother Goose*. Just shows what the world's coming to.'

Mrs Bandler was as worried as Mr Bandler, for if he did not get a goose part, it would mean a poor Christmas for the four Bandler children. However, it was no good making Mr Bandler more depressed than he was already.

'Never say die. Tell you what, if you don't get a goose, we'll let Rene go for an audition for panto. She'll be turned twelve just in time. She might get picked for a little part, she's a lovely dancer.'

Bert made a snorting, disapproving sound. He was not the first goose impersonator in his family; his father had been one and his grandfather before that, and he thought nothing of dancing; footwork should be done wearing yellow stockings and a goose's webbed feet – or there was nothing to it.

Irene was the eldest Bandler; she did not want to be mean, but she could not help hoping no goose part would turn up, so that they could stay at home in London. She talked about it to Tom, who was ten.

'Of course I know Dad needs the work and all that, but if he doesn't get a goose it would be marvellous for me, because Madame told me that if I didn't have to go away at Christmas, she thought she might get me a solo.'

Tom made a sound not unlike his father's snort. Tom was being trained by his father to be a goose, and, like his father, thought that giving a fine performance as a goose was the greatest form of stage art.

'Dance!' he said, 'In some silly panto without a goose in it? Anyway, what good would it be? You wouldn't earn enough to give us a decent Christmas. You think what Margaret-Rose and Sid eat at ordinary times, let alone Christmas day.'

Irene did not answer. It was dreadfully true. The twins, Margaret-Rose and Sid, were the biggest eaters for people of six that Effie Bandler had ever seen; and she was pretty experienced about eaters of six because, as being a comedian most of the year and a goose at Christmas was a precarious way of earning money, she had a safe way of earning it, cooking for a school.

Bert had decided that hope was dead, there would be no goose for him that year. Irene, with shining eyes, had told Madame, who taught her dancing, that she would be able to go to auditions, for they would be at home in London for Christmas. Then the telegram came. It was from a town in the north called Oldfort and said: 'Fire destroyed ogre's castle unable therefore put on puss so reviving goose opening Christmas day wire if free. Todger.'

As Bert knew the goose's part backwards, it was not necessary for him to rehearse for long, so it was exactly a week before Christmas that the Bandlers travelled up to Oldfort. They had a railway carriage to themselves, which was lucky; some people might have found them odd fellow-passengers. Bert, not having been a goose for a year, and with a rehearsal to face in the morning, considered he ought to practise. All the way from London to Oldfort, he was being a goose up and down the carriage. The twins felt very going-away-for-Christmas-ish and between eating – and they did a lot of that – they sang carols. Tom stood on the seat and gave his father criticism and advice.

'You didn't do the walk up-stage that way last year. It was slower-like and sadder.'

'Oh, Dad, that's good. Do remember that. It won't half make the audience laugh.'

Effie Bandler did not talk much, nor did Irene. Effie was going over and over what looked like pages of arithmetic, which was the family accounts. They did not make nice reading. It had been a bad year. Bert had not been engaged often as a comedian and all the money they had was Mrs Bandler's savings. Those, by the time they reached Oldfort, would not do more than pay their landlady one week's rent and keep them in very plain food. Bert would not get his first pay packet until the Friday after Christmas.

Irene looked out of the window, swallowing hard, trying not to cry. It was lovely for Dad that he had got a goose after all but, oh dear, if only she could have taken an engagement; there was quite a chance she would have been picked to dance at least a step or two alone. Imagine the glory!

Oldfort was not an attractive town. A black fog hung over it most of the time, the streets were long, grey and dismal, and mostly it rained. One thing, however, made it a lovely place in which to spend Christmas. It had the most Christmassy shops that the children had ever seen. Christmas trees blazed, Father Christmases smiled and beckoned; there was holly, mistletoe, and balloons everywhere, and in some shops gramophones playing carols and peals of bells.

Two mornings before Christmas day, as soon as breakfast was over, Effie called the family together for a conference.

'Mr Todger has subbed your father two weeks' salary.'

Bert nodded. 'Always a gentleman is Fred Todger. "It's a pleasure, Bert," he said. "You take the money and give your kids a good Christmas."'

Effie Bandler's worried creases were smoothing out. 'So we will, too. We'll get everything today – Christmas Eve is always a rush, let alone us all invited to your dress rehearsal. Now hush, children, while I read the list. Have I forgotten anything?'

It was spending frenzy, and the last shop was shutting before, loaded with parcels, the family staggered home.

'Oh, Mum,' said Margaret-Rose, 'I wish it was Christmas tomorrow. I can almost feel turkey in my mouth.'

Sid skipped at the niceness of that thought. 'And I can feel plum pudding. I can feel it sticking like it does.'

Laughing and excited, they reached home and climbed the stairs. In the doorway of their sitting-room they stood still, silenced by what they saw. On the couch, his face a queer greyish colour, lay Bert. His eyes were shut.

Effie dropped her parcels and ran to him. 'Bert! Bert, what's up?'

Bert opened his eyes. 'Hullo, me old dear. It's my foot. I slipped coming home. I think I've broken it.'

Effie patted his arm. 'I daresay it's not as bad as that. Tom, slip out and find a doctor, but don't let the landlady hear you. We don't want talk at the theatre before there's any need.'

Bert had not broken a bone, but he had torn some ligaments and, as far as the Bandlers were concerned, one was as bad as the other.

'You can't walk on that foot for at least a couple of weeks,' the doctor said, and Bert could not argue because to him his foot felt as though he would never walk on it again.

When the doctor was gone there was a nasty silence. Even the twins knew how serious the position was.

Effie said, 'If only we hadn't done the shopping today, we wouldn't have touched Mr Todger's money. Silly, I was, but I didn't want to leave it till tomorrow on account of your dress rehearsal.'

Bert raised himself on his elbow. 'Would you think I had better write to Mr Todger to tell him I can't work, or would you go, Effie?'

Effie was still in her outdoor things. She re-buttoned her coat. 'I'll go, dear. Oh, this is a business! If only you were older, Tom boy, you could take your Dad's place.'

It was then the idea came. Not all at once. Slowly, the eyes of the family turned towards Irene.

'Not the build, of course,' said Bert, 'and trained wrong. Still, a nice mover, and moving is half of the goose business.'

Effie stared at her daughter. 'You're only pint-sized, Bert, so I could fix the goose costume for her.'

'I'll help you rehearse,' Tom offered. 'I know the business just as well as Dad does. Oh, if only I was twelve!'

'Won't Mr Todger mind having Rene instead of Dad?' asked Margaret-Rose.

Mr Bandler looked at Mrs Bandler, who looked at Tom, who looked at Irene.

Then he said, 'I don't like it, but we owe two weeks' money and we've got to find it somehow. It's deceitful, I know, but we won't say anything. We'll just hope he thinks Rene is me? Now, off to bed, Rene, you have got a lot of work to get through tomorrow.'

The dress rehearsal was at half past two. From early morning, the Bandlers were busy. The twins, because nobody else could be spared, had to be trusted to do the housework. Effie went to the theatre. She was to spread the idea that Bert had a bad cold so that he couldn't speak, and for warmth he would travel to the theatre in a taxi, already dressed as a goose.

'Though how I'll get my tongue round a tale like that I don't know,' Effie said. 'Dressing at home! As if you would for a hundred colds.'

'You'll manage,' Bert comforted her. 'The great thing is to get my goose togs here as soon as you can so you can fix them for young Rene. And don't forget, I can't speak, which, seeing I won't be in the theatre, is the truth.'

'That may be,' said Effie, 'but it's a white lie and I don't hold with lies, no matter how white.'

Irene had a hard morning. First she had to learn every bit of business Bert did as a goose, and there was a great deal of it, including a long, sad piece of mimed acting which was done to music. Presently, when Effie panted home with the goose clothes, she had to rehearse wearing them. All the Bandler children knew more or less how the goose worked; strings moved its beak, eyelids, wings and tail. But knowing more or less and pulling the right strings on the right cues, shut up in a goose casing, were two very different things. Irene was a clever girl with a good memory, but before she got the goose business even nearly right she could gladly have thrown the goose clothes out of the window. Then came the worst part, the legs. By an easy adjustment, Effie had made the casing hold on to Irene, but the legs were different. The yellow tights were far too big, and the yellow webbed feet fell off each time she took a step, and when she tried wearing them over her shoes her feet were too clumsy for the movements she had to make. Effie took in the tights, and though they were wrinkled and looked rather bunchy, they would pass, but nobody could at first think what to do about the feet. It was Irene herself who solved the problem.

'I believe I could make them hold on if I wore my own tights and ballet shoes inside. My ballet shoes wouldn't be too heavy.'

It was true, she could. But holding the feet on was

only half the battle. Bert and Tom thought her foot-work terrible.

'You're a goose, dear, not Margot Fonteyn,' Bert moaned. 'You want to walk flat and a bit squashy-like.'

Tom gave a demonstration. 'Like this, Rene. Like a goose does when it's walking in a farmyard looking for food.'

Irene tried desperately hard, but there was nothing really gooselike about the way her feet moved. Bert groaned and moaned.

'Whatever dancing you do, it won't be miming, that's clear to see. All we can hope is Fred Todger's so busy with the rest of the company he won't have much time to look at you. If he thinks your work funny we must hope he'll think it's just that I'm not feeling so good with my cold.'

Effie took Irene to the theatre. It was difficult to get her into the taxi wearing her goose costume. Both Effie and the taxi driver had to push. The driver said, 'Could do with you for me Christmas dinner.'

Effie and Irene did not speak on the drive. Effie would have liked to say something encouraging and loving but it was difficult to be encouraging and loving to a daughter shut up inside a goose costume which meant she could only speak to her through a little gauze window. Just before the taxi reached the stage door, she patted the bunchy, yellow tights, knowing that Irene's legs were inside them. In answer, Irene pulled the string that worked the eye nearest to her mother. The eye winked twice. The winking meant to say, 'Don't worry,' but to Effie it said, 'Oh, Mum, I'm scared stiff. Are you?'

'I know she'll do her best,' Effie thought as she went to the front of the house to wait for her other children. 'But as a goose she's not a patch on her Dad and I don't see how Mr Todger can fail to see something's wrong. If he does, we've to pay back that sub, and what's to keep us until Bert can work again I just don't know.'

The pantomime was opened by the chorus dressed as villagers singing a song about it being a holiday. Irene was too nervous to wait in her father's dressing-room. She walked up and down the back of the stage, reminding herself what she had to do. 'That's where I sit down and lay the golden egg.' 'That's where I go to sleep.' 'That's where I flap my wings and run.' At intervals, members of the cast came up to her and slapped her goose framework and, leaning towards her muslin window, whispered, 'Sorry about the cold, Bert, old man.'

Luck was with Irene. There was trouble about the scenery. One piece jammed and held the others up. Fred Todger prided himself on the smoothness of his dress rehearsals. He sent for his stage carpenter and for much of the first half of the programme they worked together on a new plan for hanging the scenery. Being a dress rehearsal, the cast were busy on their own lines, exits, entrances, and changes of costume, and had no time to bother with anybody else. The comedian, who was on the stage a lot with the goose, did say to the principal boy, 'Bert must have a shocking cold. He's slow today. He almost forgot that business where he kicks me,' but that was all. Irene heard the curtain fall on the first half of the pantomime, and inside the goose costume she clasped her hands. 'It's half over. If only, oh if only nothing goes wrong in the second half won't it be gorgeous! Won't Dad be pleased!'

The second half was the hardest for the goose. It was where the sad miming to music came when she was alone on the stage. It was while Irene was doing this that Fred Todger first noticed something. His publicity man was sitting by him. He nudged him.

'Look at Bert Bandler. Moving his feet about queer, isn't he?'

The publicity man agreed. 'Got a nasty cold, I hear.'

Fred snorted. 'I'll have a look at him before he goes home. May have got flu. Better have a doctor.'

The Bandlers were sitting in the row just behind Mr Todger. Tom gave his mother a dig with his elbow.

'He's going to look at her! What will Rene do?'

Effie, though her heart was beating twice as fast as usual, gave Tom's knee a comforting pat. 'Ssh. We'll get Rene away before he has time to see her.'

Fred Todger was a noticing man. Having noticed how queerly the goose was lifting her feet, he began to notice other things.

'I don't know,' he whispered to the publicity man, 'but there's something altogether different about Bert's goose today. Can't put my finger on it, but I know there's something.'

Mrs Bandler pulled Tom towards her so that she could whisper into his ear. 'As soon as they start the palace scene, slip out and get a taxi. I've told Rene to make straight for the stage door. Maybe she'll miss Mr Todger.'

The pantomime ended as all pantomimes end, in a palace with a grand staircase running from high up at the back down the centre of the stage. All the cast had to march down the stairs, which gave the audience a nice chance to show by their clapping which performer they liked best. Irene, who had no idea Mr Todger had his eye on her, was so glad that the rehearsal was almost over that she hummed as she climbed the steps at the back of the stage to make her entrance on the grand staircase. It was because she was so happy that she stopped trying hard with her feet. Instead of walking in the flat, squashy way her father had tried to teach her, as nearly as she could in goose feet, she danced. Dancing in goose feet on a long flight of stairs is not a good idea. In a moment, one goose foot trod on the other. There was a crash and the goose was rolling over and over, all down the stairs on to the stage.

Irene – tangled up with the strings that worked the goose, with one goose foot turned back-to-front and giddy from rolling so fast down the stairs – could not at first get up. She heard voices.

'Give him air.' 'Are you hurt, old man?' 'Can I give you a hand up, Bert, old boy?' Then, above all the other voices, Mr Todger's roar: 'Take that goose case off him one of you.'

That brought Irene to her senses. She tried to get up and go to her place on the stage, but the back-to-front goose foot tripped her and she fell over again. She felt hands fumbling with the fastening of her goose casing. She felt it coming undone. She felt it being lifted. She was dazzled by the bright lights. There was a gasp. Then an awful silence. Everybody held their breath, waiting for Mr Todger to speak.

Mr Todger looked at Irene. She seemed very small, for she was wearing only the minute briefs she wore under her practice dancing tunic, and a sleeveless cotton blouse. Because she did not like the silence and being looked at, for something to do Irene pulled off her yellow goose tights and the goose feet. In her own tights and ballet shoes she felt more herself. She stood up and faced Mr Todger. She did not speak very loud, for she was too frightened, but she spoke clearly and bravely. She finished, ' . . . and please don't be angry with Dad. Honestly it was mostly paying you back the two weeks' money made us think of it.'

Mr Todger was staring at Irene's feet.

'You a dancer?'

'Yes.'

Mr Todger turned and roared at the orchestra. 'Play something. Want to see her dance.'

Irene did not feel a bit like dancing. She was a bit

shaky from rolling down the stairs. It seemed to her very odd of Mr Todger to want her to dance, for there was no dancing part vacant in the pantomime. Still, if Mr Todger wanted to see her dance, she must dance. She asked the orchestra to play a waltz, held an attitude, then raised herself on to her points.

Irene was well trained, talented, and far more of a dancer than any Mr Todger had engaged for his pantomimes. So much so that she quite took his breath away and he did not, when her dance was over, speak at once. Irene misread his silence. She stooped, picked up the goose costume, the yellow tights, and the feet.

'I'm sorry about spoiling your rehearsal. I'll go now.'

A roar from Mr Todger stopped her. 'Where d'you think you're going? You stay here.' He turned to his stage manager. 'Reset the stage for the pool of youth in the magic wood. Tell the wardrobe mistress I want her. I'm going to do something never done before in *Mother Goose*. It's not only the dame the pool makes young. I'm going to have a goose who jumps into it and comes out a young, dancing gosling. How's that? And what a Press! "Daughter takes place of her injured father."

You're engaged, kid. You can play the goose as long as your Dad's laid up, though you're not much of a hand at it, and when he's better you'll stop on and dance as the gosling. What do you say?'

Irene was so happy she felt she would burst. To help by being the goose was lovely, but to dance as a gosling! A tu-tu, perhaps of yellow feathers. It was too much.

She was saved trying to answer because Effie cried, 'Bless you, Mr Todger!'

skating to

the Stars

William and Joanna met at the top of the stairs. Joanna leant over the banister to see that neither their father nor mother were within hearing distance. She put lips close to William's ear.

'Try to look awfully pleased and Christmassy. They mind awfully and they mustn't know how much we mind.'

William had been going to say exactly that to Joanna. Nothing is more aggravating than to be full of good intentions which you intend to pass on, and instead find someone giving the good intentions to you first, and it's especially annoying when the speaking first comes from a twin sister. He gave her a push.

'Don't whisper, you're tickling my ear. It didn't take you to think of that. I've been thinking it all night.'

'I hope you haven't, or we'll never do our spins. I dreamt I got to the rink with only one skate.'

'What did we do?'

Joanna followed him downstairs.

'Awfully well really, like you do in dreams. We worked out a whole programme where I never used anything but my left foot, and do you know, we came out top!'

William giggled. 'That's the sort of idiotic thing you do in dreams. I dreamt that there wasn't any ice and we were skating in water.'

'If you were awake all night, how did you dream?'

Their mother called to them from the dining room. 'Come on, you two. Your train goes in an hour.'

The children's father, Mr Biddle, was a vet. He was always rather a thin, anxious-looking chap, but lately he had been looking especially thin and anxious. It had been a year when animals had kept in extraordinarily good health. Dogs seemed to be brought to him only for inferior things like having their toe-nails cut, which you can't charge much for, and he had scarcely seen a cat in months. He looked sadder than ever as he kissed the twins good morning.

'Yes, for goodness' sake don't miss the train. That really would be the end.'

Mrs Biddle tried to help, but she was not a good actress, and her voice had an 'England expects that every man' tone. 'The Biddles are never downhearted, are they?'

Mr Biddle and the two children felt worse than they had before. William poured some milk on to his porridge.

'Joanna and I aren't downhearted. Obviously we can't go on having expensive skating lessons if enough beastly dogs don't get ill to pay for them, but knowing you can't have a thing and being awfully bright and saying, "I'm so glad you can't afford to pay for more skating lessons" is two different things.'

Joanna stretched a hand across to her mother and laid it on her arm. 'He's quite right, Mummy. I know you mean well but we don't need encouraging to be brave.'

Mrs Biddle swallowed and poured out Joanna's tea. 'I only put that voice on because I'm so nearly crying. When I think you got your silver medals long before your fourteenth birthdays and are good enough to go in for an open championship while you're still only fourteen and then it all has to stop, it seems such a waste.'

Mr Biddle helped himself to a piece of toast. 'I'm not so sure it's a waste. I don't suppose there'd have been much future in it, especially for William. Better really he comes to work with me.'

William put down his porridge spoon and looked at his father in shocked amazement. 'I don't want to be rude or anything like that, but Joanna and I would probably have got our gold medals and one day been the European Pair Champions and afterwards the World Pair Champions, and then we could have turned pros and earned a fortune, which would mean that when I marry and have children, I wouldn't have to say, "I'm sorry you can't skate any more because no beastly dog has had distemper."'

Mr Biddle shook his head. 'That's all very fine and large, but there are a lot of mights about it, and you know I always did say that I didn't think much of it as a career.'

Joanna raised her eyebrows. 'Did you? It seems to Miss Joanna Biddle that she heard you say to the doctor that the sooner we were pros, the better.'

Mr Biddle swallowed the last of his tea. 'Quite right, Joanna, but I feel badly about this. I've racked my brains to find a way, and there just isn't one. The higher up you go in this skating business, the more expensive it becomes and it just can't be done.'

He got up. 'Goodbye, my dears, bless you both and very good luck for today.'

Mrs Biddle waited until the door closed before she spoke. 'He doesn't mean to be cross. He's thought of everything, but it's impossible, so it's no good talking about it. I only wish I could come with you both today, but it would only add to the expense; anyway, I'll have a very nice supper waiting for you when you come in.'

'I wish you could come,' said Joanna. 'After the championship they told us some of the artists who are going to be in the skating pantomime might be going to rehearse. I hope they do. I can't imagine *Puss in Boots* on ice, can you? Max Lindblom will be Puss. He's absolutely marvellous, we saw pictures of him once.'

Mrs Biddle looked at the clock.

'Eat up, dears, you haven't much time. I've just got to put your sandwiches in paper and put them in the corner of your cases. Be sure to eat them, won't you? Don't get into a dream watching the other skaters and bring them home again.'

William and Joanna had often been in for tests and competitions, but today was different from all the other tests and competition days. They were each always nervous in their own way. William's way was what he called 'feeling Jack-in-the-boxish'. He said it was as if there was a Jack-in-the-box inside him, and every time he thought about skating, the lid popped open and Jack jumped out. Joanna's way was to feel sick, the sort of sick you feel in a lift that goes down too fast. She never was sick, and always stopped feeling sick the moment she got on to the ice, but she was never absolutely certain that she would not be. Today, because it was the last time they would ever enter for a skating competition, they felt miserable as well as nervous.

As soon as the train started, William said, 'My box is much bigger than usual, and Jack comes out more often, and every time he comes out he hits me inside with his hard little hands.'

Joanna gulped. 'Don't. I was trying not to think of

my inside – it feels awful, it's the kind of day when I'm almost sure I might be.'

'Not here,' said William. 'It says the fine is five pounds to spit, so I should think it's twenty-five pounds at least to be sick. I suppose it depends how much. I wonder if they measure it.'

Joanna gave a moan. 'Don't, William. Do talk of something else, or I will be. Honestly I will.'

William looked at her. She certainly was a very odd colour – the sort of colour the leaves of a bulb are when it is first brought out of a cellar. He found it difficult to think quickly because of his Jack-in-the-box, but suddenly he remembered that in three weeks it would be Christmas.

'Do you suppose there would be enough money for us to go and see *Puss in Boots?*'

Joanna forgot her inside for a moment.

'Oh, I wonder. I wish we'd asked before we started. If we knew absolutely for certain we were seeing *Puss in Boots*, saying goodbye to Miss Brown and everybody wouldn't be so bad. It would be seeing skating anyway, and that's better than no skating at all.'

William and Joanna were not the first arrivals at the

rink. Several pairs were standing about, waiting for the warm-up before the competition began. Many of them the children knew by sight, and a few of them to speak to. The skaters said good morning to the children and smiled kindly, for not only were they the youngest entrants, but not severe competitors, as it was their first appearance in an open championship and they were not likely to get high marks.

Joanna examined, though trying not to stare, the competitors' clothes. She was very interested in what they wore. Her own idea of what she would like to wear was a short, flared rose-pink frock, with ballet frills underneath of blue. What she was wearing was a brown velvet frock with white collar and cuffs, and brown velvet briefs to match. All the other women skaters had tights. Joanna had wanted tights ever since she had her first pair of skates, which was when she was four. Now that she was fourteen she had got used to not having tights, but she still envied all the other legs wearing them, not only because they looked smart, but because they hid the pink-and-blue-in-patches look tightless legs got before they were properly warmed up. William wore brown too – a brown jersey and brown trousers. Joanna thought he looked nice; they both had coppery-coloured hair which went well with brown, but she had a feeling that while William looked sensible and athletic in his clothes, she looked rather mouse-like in hers.

Their instructor, Miss Brown, came over to them. Usually she was wearing skating clothes, and looked slim and pretty, but today she had on a long teddy-bear coat, large boots, wool gloves, and was carrying a rug.

'Hullo twins. How's your Jack-in-the-box, William?'

'Terrible. He comes out more often than usual.'

'And I was nearly sick on the train, and I still might be.'

Miss Brown laughed and opened her bag.

'I must say, you do look a little as if you'd had a rough crossing, Joanna.' She took a box of rouge from her bag. 'Turn your face up, I'll put on some make-up. William, look in my bag and you'll find some glucose sweets. That'll soon put you both straight.' She stood away from Joanna with her head on one side, 'Very nice, too, Miss Redhead. I like that Alice-in-Wonderland ribbon round your hair.'

Joanna looked down at herself. 'Don't you think I

look awfully little-girlish? I wish I had frills that stuck out. I seem so flat everywhere, I haven't even any chest.'

Miss Brown sighed. 'You're very nice as you are. I am mad you two have to give up skating, but mind you, I'm not saying die yet, I always believe there may be miracles for everybody round the corner.' She saw a movement of the other skaters. 'I'd better go and get a seat, you'll be starting soon.'

William and Joanna had never been able to make up their minds which was the best position in which to be drawn in a competition. They did not like being first because they felt the judges would not have set-tled down, and they did not like being last because the judges might be bored. This time they were drawn about the middle.

'I don't like that,' said William. 'That means we will be just before they've had a sandwich, in which case they'll be hungry and cross, and if we come after they've eaten, they'll feel fat and sleepy and won't watch us properly.'

Joanna shivered. She did not bother to answer William; when his Jack-in-the-box got obstreperous it made him say truculent things. He was the opposite to her. When her inside heaved and she felt most as if she were in a dropping lift, she could not say anything at all. She supposed it was natural, really. Obviously it was safer to keep your mouth shut for feeling sick, but unnecessary for Jacks, which did not try to leave their boxes.

It was a relief to them both when the band struck up and they and the other competitors were allowed on the ice for a warm-up. They always did the most difficult and the most space-taking things during a warm-up, for they had learned by experience that the more of the rink they took up and the faster they moved, the sooner they got rid of William's Jack-in-the-box and Joanna's lift feeling. They skated hand in hand to the bottom of the rink, took split jumps away from each other, and then, with William spread-eagled and Joanna holding a good arabesque, they curved almost the whole length of the rink, then broke apart for spins, spirals and jumps, which took them all the way back again. Perhaps because they were the youngest competitors, or perhaps because they were so obviously twins, with their green eyes and red hair, the people watching clapped them, and clapping, as Joanna whispered to William, even if it wasn't because people liked your skating, but only because they were being kind because you were young, was very encouraging.

William, warm and cheerful, agreed with her. 'Death to any Jacks.'

As soon as the warm-up period was over, the children took good seats from which to watch the other competitors and yet be ready when it came to their own turn. They carefully studied the judges. There were five of them: three men and two women. It was difficult unless you looked at them carefully to see which were the men and which were the women, for they all wore trousers, and the two women judges wore their hair cut short, rather like the men. Their bodies could not help looking the same because they were all stuffed with jerseys, over which they wore large, warm overcoats, and the feet of all five were in enormous fur-lined boots. The children, after one look at them, called them after their numbers, which were tied to their backs.

'I have a feeling,' Joanna whispered, 'that I am not going to like Four. I never like a judge that does that sort of angry dancing up and down to keep its feet warm.'

William was scowling. 'It's Two I'm going to hate. Two's going to be the sort that looks grand, bored and uninterested, and only gets excited when it comes to giving fewer marks than any of the other judges.'

The music struck up. The twins were silent, completely absorbed. Watching skating competitions is fun for everybody, but when you are a skater and can tell when a step or a figure is well performed and a programme well chosen, watching is thrilling. William and Joanna always played the same game at competitions and championships. Each of them pretended to be a judge and gave the skater or skaters the marks they thought they would win, and the one that had the most correct answers by the end of the day had the right to claim the next treat going in the family.

As the skaters finished, Joanna said, 'Four point eight.'

William disagreed. 'Lucky if they get four point one. I thought it was a terrible programme, not enough variety. I bet they lose marks for that.'

The judges agreed with William. As each held up their cards, the figure in one hand and the decimal points in the other, he grinned at Joanna.

'What did I tell you – look at Two's figures. Did you see the gloating look he gave when he saw he'd given fewer marks than anybody else?'

'I was looking at Four,' Joanna whispered. 'I told you Four would mark meanly and I was right.'

The twins so enjoyed watching the other competitors that they were sorry when it got near their turn and they had to go to the cloakroom to spruce themselves up, but they were back in time to see the whole performance of the pair before them. These were a young married couple called Kingdom, last year's winners defending their title. William and Joanna had never spoken to the Kingdoms except to say good morning, but at home they were always talking about them. The Kingdoms were their ideal, the sort of pair skaters that they had hoped some day to be, if only enough dogs had gone on being ill to pay for their lessons.

Joanna looked admiringly at Mrs Kingdom's white tailored outfit.

'Doesn't she look gorgeous? Of course I know it wouldn't make me skate better, but I do know it would help if I could wear that sort of dress.'

Miss Brown was standing behind them. 'It wouldn't help a bit, Joanna, and you know it. I hope those two keep their title. It's the last time they will compete: they're turning professional. They're doing a cat and dog dance in *Puss in Boots*.'

Joanna gazed even more admiringly at the champion pair.

'How splendiferous for them,' William said. 'I bet they'll be good.'

Miss Brown nodded. 'So do I. I believe they're going to rehearse after we've finished, so if you hang around, you might see them.'

The couple before the Kingdoms were on had finished. They skimmed backwards towards the Kingdoms, who were standing hand in hand, their arms outstretched, holding arabesques, and they turned to see what marks they had won. William and Joanna were not interested in their marks; their eyes were on the Kingdoms who were moving forward, ready to perform.

'I don't care what you say,' William whispered to Miss Brown, 'but it must be difficult not to think a person looks better when he's got a white suit properly tailored for him instead of a bought ready-made like mine.'

'Not to mention having your frock tailored like she has,' said Joanna. 'I know I'd feel absolutely different if I had a skirt with all those beautiful pleats.'

Miss Brown put her finger to her lips. The judges had shown their marks and were moving back to watch the Kingdoms. The conductor of the orchestra tapped his music stand and the Kingdoms stood side by side, their arms outstretched.

The Kingdoms were lovely to watch. They had arranged a difficult programme, full of spirals and jumps, but both were exquisite movers and on the ice they were more like ballet dancers than skaters, one figure sliding into the other, and the technique which made that possible beautifully disguised. Round and round they went – their programme was so swift-moving and so difficult, the children often caught their breaths.

'Ooh, what a lovely spread-eagle!' William whispered, as the pair exquisitely balanced, their arms linked, gliding down the rink for their finale. As Kingdom lifted Mrs Kingdom above his head and held her there in a split position, William's eyes glowed with admiration. 'They're going to finish on a death spiral, look . . . '

The Kingdoms turned, Mrs Kingdom with her back to her husband bent towards him, her arms above her head, then something went wrong. There was an infinitesimal pause, she gave a moan and dropped in a heap on the ice. There was a moment's confusion, then her husband with the assistance of another man carried her off. A babel of voices arose. William turned to Miss Brown.

'What happened?'

Miss Brown looked rather green, but she gave Joanna's frock a little twitch. 'Don't let it upset you. Just go on and skate as best you can and forget about it. It's the easiest thing in the world, to have an accident doing the death spiral – the timing has to be perfect – but you're not doing a death spiral, so don't worry about it. You just think of yourselves, and do as well as you possibly can.'

That was easier said than done: the Kingdoms were not just any skaters. They were the twins' special skaters. Joanna had tears in her eyes.

'Do you think she's badly hurt?'

Miss Brown managed to sound very confident. 'Just a little sprain I should think. It was probably painful and she fainted. Now off you go, and don't disgrace me.'

The twins did not own band parts which were expensive, but used gramophone records. They were to skate to Waldteufel's 'Skater's Waltz'. It was quite impossible to worry about the Kingdoms or anybody or anything else as the first notes of their music reached them over the loudspeakers. Miss Brown had arranged a good programme for them, but well within their abilities. Had

each figure been done as well by both of them as they had sometimes done them at their practice and lessons, they would have got very high marks indeed, but a combination of figures and movements lasting four minutes and done at great speed could not all turn out perfectly. It was too much to hope. They made several mistakes all the way through, bad changes of edge, awkward lifts, incorrect positions – but for a four-minute programme, it was the best all-round effort the twins had ever made. They finished on a drag and came back to Miss Brown hot and triumphant. She put an arm round each.

'Very nice, my pets. It makes me more savage than ever to think you've got to give up. Let's see what the grand panjandrums are going to award you.'

There was the usual pause while the judges fumbled for the figures and decimal points in the boxes which held them, then they raised the cards above their heads. Miss Brown murmured the figures.

'There,' said William, 'I told you Two would hate us.'

Joanna looked severely at Four. 'And I told you Four would mark meanly.'

Miss Brown was amused. 'And I tell you that One, Three and Five have marked generously – far better than I'd hoped.' She saw the judges were moving off and the band getting up. 'You had better eat your lunch. I'm just off to get mine.'

The twins put on their coats and with their lunch packets in their hands settled down in good seats to watch the rest of the competitors. They had not been there long when a sad-faced little man came and sat beside them. He looked so forlorn that Joanna felt embarrassed to go on eating. It was like eating while watching a road accident.

'Do you think he's hungry?' she whispered to William. 'Ought I to give him a sandwich?'

William leant forward and, pretending to have a look at Joanna's sandwiches, peered at the man. Then he sat back in his seat.

'He doesn't look a very sandwichy sort, but if you offer him one, I'll give you half of one of mine to make up.'

Joanna held out her packet to the man. 'Would you care for a sandwich, or have you had your lunch?'

The man seemed to come back from a very long way off. 'You made me jump. I was thinking of something else. No, thank you, I'm too upset to eat and that's a fact.'

Joanna looked at him sympathetically. 'I'm sorry, I know exactly how you feel. I was upset last summer. It was bad fish. I felt peculiar for days and days.'

'It's not my stomach. It's Mrs Kingdom. I've been after those two the best part of a year.' He turned fiercely to Joanna. 'What did they want to put that death spiral in for? There were plenty of other things they could have done.'

William sprang to the Kingdoms' defence. 'It's very difficult to do. It's the sort of thing any pair would put in their programme if they could do it.'

Joanna thought the man looked too miserable to be cross with him. 'What did you want the Kingdoms for?'

'For the boss. He saw them and he said to me, "Sid," he said, "Get those Kingdoms for Puss."'

Joanna misunderstood him. She had often heard her mother say, 'Run and buy me some fish for puss,' but why would any puss want the Kingdoms and what for? She said politely in a very inquiring way, 'Puss?'

'*Puss in Boots.* There was going to be a run-through for the Kingdoms after. Specially fixed, it had been. Got all the girls along. Now look what's happened.'

William tried to be comforting. 'I daresay she'll be

all right in a day or two. I've sprained my ankles and they didn't take awfully long to get well, and Joanna sprained hers terribly badly once and hurt a ligament, and even that didn't take long.'

Sid gave William a pitying look. 'Sprained ankle! Did it look like a sprained ankle? Why, you could hear it crack. It's broken, that's what it is. Directly they got her to the hospital they knew. It's being x-rayed, but it's a break all right. The boss is in a proper state. Dancing the special cat and dog turn, they were, the big spectacular number. I don't know who's going to replace them.'

Joanna felt so miserable for him she laid a hand on his arm. 'I'm awfully sorry for you, but I expect you'll find somebody else – but, of course, nobody as good as the Kingdoms. Nobody is as good as the Kingdoms. They'd have held the championship for certain, if she hadn't had that accident.'

Sid seemed comforted by Joanna's little pat. He turned for the first time and looked at them.

'That's right, very hard to find anyone as good as those two. That's why the boss . . . ' he broke off and stared first at Joanna and then at William. 'You were the last couple that skated, the red-headed twins.

Now, wait a moment, don't speak, Sid's thinking. You answer questions and that's all you need to do. First, how old are you?'

'Fourteen and seven months,' said William.

'At school?'

Joanna was surprised at his ignorance. 'Of course. You have to be when you're fourteen.'

Sid nodded. He sounded gloomy again. 'I'll tell you the rest. You're Dad and Mum's pride and hope. Silver medallists. Entered for open British Championship at fourteen and expected to win it in a year or two. Likely to get gold medals next year. Plans for the future – the European Championship and one day the World.' William opened his mouth to answer, but Sid stopped him. 'Don't interrupt, no need to tell me; I've told you.'

Joanna gave Sid's arm another little pat. 'We must interrupt. You see, you were quite right about it all, but it isn't going to happen now. It's been a very healthy year for dogs.'

'Dogs! Who's talking about dogs?'

In a rush, the twins told him their story. They explained about their father being a vet, and how well all dogs seemed to be lately, and they explained about this being their very last day's skating. The more they explained, the more interested Sid looked, and as an interested face is a great help to conversation, in the end he heard everything. When the children could think of nothing more to tell him, he got up.

'Phone at home?'

'Of course,' said William. 'Vets are always on the phone.'

'Ring your parents up. Tell them you may be late home. Now, don't you two dare move from this rink. I want you both the moment these competitions are over.'

Joanna, though she liked Sid, thought that was a rather ordering about way for a stranger to talk. 'What for?'

'To do the same act you did at the competition this morning, and don't ask me what for, because I don't know what for, but I've got a hunch, and when Sid's got a hunch, it's worth following.'

❄

The rink was almost empty, except for Miss Brown, Sid and Sid's boss – a large, fat, rich-looking man in a wide-shouldered overcoat, smoking a cigar. William and Joanna glided on to the ice to the music of 'The Skater's Waltz'. All the afternoon they had been lit by excitement – what could Sid be planning for them? Could it be – no, of course not – it was nonsense to suppose anyone would think of them to take the place of the Kingdoms.

Miss Brown had agreed with them. 'I wouldn't be too hopeful if I were you,' she had said. 'What I think you'll find is that they may be going to offer to use you in the ballets and give you the understudies of the cat and dog. I've heard they're planning to wire to America to see if they can get a star couple for the Kingdoms' place.'

But hopes, fears, Sid and Sid's boss were forgotten as they swung down the ice and broke away from each other for their first spin. In the aggravating way that things happen, they performed rather better this time than they had in the competition. Of course, it was very nice to have done well for Sid and the gentleman with the cigar, but it would have been nice to have done as well as that in the competition. The placings had not yet been announced, but Miss Brown thought it was possible they might come sixth, which was wonderfully higher than they had anticipated. If they had skated as well as they were doing now, it would have made their coming sixth almost a certainty. They finished their drag facing Sid and the man with the cigar, then self-consciously, because they did not know why their skating had been watched, came over to them.

It was Miss Brown who told them the news. 'This is Mr Crumsky, children, who is putting on *Puss in Boots*. He has decided to offer you the parts of the cat and dog. Isn't that lovely?'

Sid got up. 'To make quite certain that everything is above board and signed on time, I'm driving you home to your parents, pen in one hand and contract in the other.'

It was almost impossible to think of a gayer family than the Biddles were that evening. After Sid had gone with the signed contract in his pocket, Mrs Biddle said supper was ready. What a supper! All the things the children liked best to eat were on the table at the same time. Everybody spoke without bothering to find out if anybody else was listening.

'Us earning fifty pounds a week. Imagine!' said William.

Joanna gazed starry-eyed into space. 'I think if I could have chosen, absolutely chosen, what I would like to be most in a pantomime, it would have been a little white cat with roses round its neck, which is just what I'm going to be.'

Mrs Biddle was almost too happy to eat. 'It's too lovely, I feel as if I've come out of a long dark tunnel into a field of buttercups.'

Mr Biddle said the best thing of all.

'I never thought skating as a career had much future in it, but I'm bound to own you two seem to have made a good start, and one thing I must admit, it was very tactful of you to pick those parts. Maybe it's an omen that there are better times coming for me; after all, it isn't every vet who can say, 'I have two children: one is a cat, and the other is a dog.'

First publication details

'The Audition' published in *Daily Mail Annual for Boys and Girls* (1949)

'The Moss Rose' published in *Every Girl's Annual* (1950)

'The Chain' published in the *Radio Times* (1950)

'Thimble' read on radio by May Jenkin on 29 December 1949. Published in *Uncle Mac's Children's Hour Story Book* (1951)

'The Bells Keep Twelfth Night' published in *BBC Children's Hour Annual* (1951)

'The Pantomime Goose' published in *Daily Mail Annual for Boys and Girls* (1951)

'Skating to the Stars' published in *Daily Mail Annual for Boys and Girls* (1952)

'The Princess' published in *Dancers, Dancers, Dancers*, edited by Lee Wyndham (1961)